Wrecker Jack

By

G. Fleming

ILLUSTRATED

BY

LUIS HO

DEDICATED TO

JAMIE, JENNY & BEN

COVER DESIGN BY

SHANNEN ASHCROFT

– Chapter 1 –

THE DREAM

Jay was being haunted by nightmares. Dreams of black storms, broken ships and crashing waves from two hundred years ago - dreadful, confusing and frightening - relentlessly returning nightly since he arrived in Cornwall four nights ago.

..... He was on a blustery freezing beach at night, a terrifying storm raging around him and the dark outline of a wrecked ship looming and rocking nearby. Pitch black and icy cold - Jay could only see shades of black and grey, and the outlines of shadowy figures. The deafening crashing of waves breaking onto rocks surrounded him and the terrible screams of men and women drowning or being murdered roared in his ears.

He tried to run away through the blackness, leaving the sounds of the sea behind. He was running blind on a stony beach. The pebbles felt hard and slippery beneath his bare feet. The beach was a mass of shadows. It was so dark, that unless someone moved or shouted, you could not tell them apart from the rocks or wreckage.

In the dark chaos, Jay was just able to distinguish three different kinds of sounds; the murderers and thieves cursing, those crying out for help, and those trying desperately to save them. A heaving mass of the best and worst of human kind - thrown into a storm in a black hurricane and left to fight for survival.

The water from the gale and sea had soaked him through in a minute as he battled against wind, rain, stinging sand and icy wet clothes, trying to reach the nearby cave. He tripped over someone on the floor, a hand reached up to him, bloody and wounded, but when Jay turned back to help, the man was gone – Where? How?

A woman screamed – just one of the shadows, and the cries of the lost and fallen just kept getting louder and the crashing of water onto rocks and the splintering of the smashed ship became overwhelming as he pressed his frozen hands to his ears to try to block it all out.

There was a small cave in front of him, a tiny flickering light just inside. Lying face down on the damp floor was the body of a large man, and towering over him a larger dark figure holding a knife. Jay ran up to the shadowy figures, but just as the light was about to shine on their faces, everything went black and silent.....

Jay sat bolt upright in bed. He was sweating and out of breath as if he had been running hard. The dream was so real and clear, the terrible screams still echoing in his ears, but most of all he was angry and frustrated that once again he had failed to see the faces of the figures in the cave.

His bedroom was as dark as the dream. Pushing sweat-matted chestnut brown hair out of his eyes, Jay gazed out of the window to the cliffs and the distant sea. The lighthouse silently blinked its warning to the incoming ships reflecting in his deep brown eyes, and in the gentle breeze of a quiet night, the splashing of the waves were now peaceful and comforting.

When Jay woke again at seven in the morning he felt better. The dream had not returned, and the small attic bedroom was filled with bright, warm sunlight. Throwing back the covers, he quickly dressed into a baggy t-shirt, jeans and trainers and ran downstairs to find something to eat.

4

Everyone was still asleep. Jay grabbed some biscuits and a bottle of water and strolled out into the small garden overlooking the sea. As the salty, cool breeze caught his face, the dream came back vividly to him, and above the call of the circling seagulls, he remembered the nightmare cry from the people in the freezing black sea.

Jay was fourteen, tall, lean, athletic and full of energy. Impulsive and brave, he had warm deep brown eyes, with strong eyebrows and a square jaw. He owned a generous wide smile with a deep, sincere laugh and elegant strong hands. Jay possessed an analytical mind – a natural problem solver and rescuer, confident, strong willed and stubborn.

He made his way down to the shore as he did most mornings. His Dad had been involved in a serious car accident three years ago and was now in a permanent coma. This tragedy had eventually led to the loss of their home and all their money. His family had recently had their house re-possessed in London and now they were staying in an aunt's cottage in Cornwall until something better came along.

There were five of them altogether, eldest Marc, twenty, was away in the armed forces, his older sister Natasha, sixteen, was staying with friends in London, Jay was the middle child at fourteen, then he had one younger brother Daniel who was twelve and a little sister Katie who was four. All now homeless and missing their life in London.

The sea was beautifully calm now, rippling blue water with silvery sprays that broke onto shining rocks, dragging along shaggy seaweed that floated in the lapping of the waves.

The shore was deserted apart from a couple of old fishermen doing something to a fishing boat that lay on its side on the pebble beach. Jay went closer, and sat nearby watching them working silently. One of the fishermen looked over at him and stared, his old weather-beaten face wrinkled like brown leather.

"You that Pengelli boy then?" the old man growled, his voice croaky and rough.

"Yes." said Jay, looking out to sea, past the old fisherman's piercing eyes.

"There's bad blood in the Pengelli's." the old man grunted, shaking his head, his few remaining grey hairs blowing about in the wind.

"What d'you mean?" Jay asked, but the second fisherman was also shaking his head,

"Aye, a lot of bad blood in *that* lot."

Jay stood up to walk away, his brown eyes flashing angrily. He wasn't going to sit there and take that, but as he turned away he heard them muttering,

"Wrecker Jack, he were the worst."

"Aye." said his friend looking up at the boy, "....so far."

– Chapter 2 –

DEN CROWLE

The name Wrecker Jack was well known to Jay; it was the name of a far distant relative from 1790, and also the name of the old Inn in the little town. He made his way there, down long twisting country lanes, in the cold Cornish morning; the sun was bright, but the chill from the air felt damp.

The narrow street was deserted. The Inn was ancient and smelt of the sea. Old black timbers and tiny lead windows made the pub appear dark and unwelcoming in the morning light - but at night, with a roaring log fire, the place came alive with loud voices and the clinking of beer glasses and drunken laughter of locals and tourists.

Jay had been peering through one of the small windows into the deserted Inn, when someone shoved him roughly on the shoulder making him jump.

"What you looking for?" A voice with a slight Cornish accent demanded. Jay turned and saw a tall lad, about his age, but he was heavy built with short-cropped hair, a freckled face and large rough looking hands.

"I was just looking." Jay replied. The other boy just stared at him. Jay stared back, trying to act casual.

"Wrecker Jack – was this his place?" Jay asked. The boy looked taken aback, he frowned at Jay,

"You wouldn't happen to be that Pengelli boy then?" the boy snarled. Jay nodded cautiously. The boy leaned over Jay, bringing his face up close to his,

"I'm Den Crowle." He whispered in a low, menacing growl, "Wrecker Jack murdered Matt Crowle in 1790. I hate Pengellis."

"What?" Said Jay, stepping back quickly. "What are you talking about, that was 200 years ago? What's that got to do with me?"

The two boys stared at each other, there were a few seconds of silence, and then Den suddenly started to laugh. His loud, joyful laugh caught Jay by surprise and made him smile despite his confusion.

"It's true though," Den was saying, as the two boys stepped into the Inn, "Wrecker Jack and Mad Matt Crowle were smugglers just down this coastline. They robbed, smuggled and murdered for years." Den led Jay through the old Inn across the original uneven stone floor. The place was deserted and silent.

Den pulled Jay over to a large dark painting hanging over the fireplace. It was the portrait of a huge, evil looking man. Everything about the figure was black – his clothes, his beard and especially his eyes.

"That's Wrecker Jack," Den said, "the most evil man ever to sail the Cornish coast," he paused to chuckle, "except, of course, for Mad Matt Crowle."

Jay was beginning to wonder how much of Matt Crowle's madness had passed down to his companion, when there were heavy footsteps behind them, and a deep, gravelly voiced bellowed out,

"Who spoke the name of Wrecker Jack in my Inn – damn his bones!" Jay jumped as a huge red headed man appeared, frowning and cursing and waving his massive fists in the air,

"May he rot in hell fire, murdering pirate!" he yelled. Jay took another step back, but Den stayed where he was, grinning at this crazy giant.

"Dad" said Den, "This is Jay Pengelli." Jay felt his heart drop into his boots, but the huge man starting to laugh, that same hearty roar of his son.

"Sorry lad" he exclaimed, "didn't mean to scare ya, it's all part of my act for the tourists." Jay smiled weakly. The giant continued,

"No offence intended. Me and Den here don't hold any grudges, even if one of yours bumped off one of my mine and then made off with all the treasure."

They were all laughing heartily, but Jay's attention was drawn to a faint, urgent knocking sound. It seemed to be coming from behind the bar....

– Chapter 3 –

WHO IS IN THE CELLAR?

"What's that?" Jay asked.

"Just the cellar door."

"No, I mean that knocking." Den and his Dad (John) looked puzzled.

"What knocking is that then? I can't hear anythin'." John said.

But the knocking grew louder and more insistent, and now it seemed that someone was rattling the door handle from inside. Jay rushed over to the old, small, black door and tried to open it.

"What 'ya doin' lad?" John was saying, following him over to the bar, "That's locked, it's just the beer cellar, there's no-one in there."

But the rattling was getting louder and now Jay could hear a young voice pleading for help.

"Someone's trapped! Quick!" Jay shouted, "Can't you hear them?"

"We can't hear nothing," Den was saying, "What you talking about?"

By now Jay was pulling frantically at the old iron door handle, but the door would not budge.

The voice behind the door was getting louder and more desperate,

"Let me out, let me out, help, please, help, help, please, PLEASE!"

Jay couldn't understand why the others were not rushing around, did not seem concerned. There was a boy locked in the cellar, a terrified boy in the dark.

"Hurry, please, please, HELP ME!" the voice was screaming in panic. From over Jay's shoulder, a large old key appeared as John leaned over him to unlock the door.

"Steady on lad" he was saying "There's nothing in there. What you gettin' in such a state about?"

The old key stuck in the lock, he struggled to turn it.

"HELP, QUICK, HELP!!" Jay was almost in tears from frustration, he grabbed the key, turned the lock and heaved open the heavy wooden door. The shouting stopped immediately, and Jay looked into his own face in the darkness, he turned to Den,

"It's a mirror!" Jay shouted.

"What is?" asked Den, puzzled. Jay turned back, only silent blackness faced him.

There was no one there. There was no mirror and no reflection. A cold, icy feeling began to clutch his stomach - he had looked into his *own* terrified face behind that door. The fear crept up his spine and caught the back of his neck like icy fingers and sent a shudder through his body. There was nothing sinister in the room; just boxes and a cold stone floor leading away down a long rough passageway.

"You'd better sit down lad," said John kindly, "you've gone as white as a ghost."

Jay sat on a stool and drank the cool water that Den handed him. He was beginning to feel foolish. The others hadn't heard a thing, and all that he had seen was himself. What did it mean?

"Feelin' better?" John asked kindly. Jay nodded.

"I thought I could hear someone trapped behind the door. I could hear them calling for help." Jay tried to explain. Den raised his eyebrows,

"You on any medication?" John asked, "does this sort of thing happen a lot then?"

Jay smiled weakly,

"No." He replied lightly – but he looked over to the battered old black door, and felt fear.

"Tell you what," John said, "When you've finished your water, we'll all go into the cellar to have a good look round, just to make sure and put your mind at rest. What d'you say?"

"Where does it go?" Jay asked, glancing back at the door.

"It's the old smuggling route," Den said, "we use it for storing beer and stuff now, but Mad Matt and Wrecker Jack used it to get down to shore when they were smuggling from the ships. One old stone passage leads down to the caves on the shore, and the other one leads to Mad Matt's house. They used them as escape routes, and to hide stuff."

John took a large old flashlight from behind the bar,

"The cellar's only lit this end, if you want to go exploring down to the shore, you'd better take a torch with you."

Jay slowly got down off the barstool. He was excited that an adventure was just beginning, but as he walked towards the entrance to the smugglers' caves, the feeling of fear continued to tug at the back of his neck.

– Chapter 4 –

THE SMUGGLERS TUNNEL

Den was laughing and joking as the three of them stepped into the cold cellar. John switched on a dim, yellow electric light, which turned the room from a dark, scary place into an ordinary looking beer cellar. Crates of bottles, wine, beer, soft drinks and boxes of crisps and peanuts were stacked everywhere.

Jay could see nothing in the room that could have caused such a complete and clear reflection, but anyway, he sure didn't imagine the shouting.

"Have some cheese and onion." John shouted as he tossed two packets of crisps at the boys.

At the back of the cellar, and also to the left hand side, there were two small doorways in the damp stone walls. Den turned on the powerful torch and shone the light down one of the passageways at the back of the cellar.

"That one leads down to the shore, just right for sneaking up in the dead of night with a few barrels of stolen brandy," laughed John.

"Old Mad Matt had the perfect set up here. He came along that passage on the left there which leads from his cottage, met Wrecker Jack here, and the two of them would go smuggling and up to no good, down the other passage to the ships waiting in the cove."

"Didn't the police know?" Jay asked.

"Weren't no police round here then, it was the Excise Men, and most of them were in the pocket of the Squire who was the biggest smuggler of them all. Anyway, you going down to see this beach or not?"

Den was already halfway into the entrance. Jay looked back at John to see if he was following, but he was standing still and shaking his head and muttering,

"You'll never get me to set my boots down that hell hole. That's where Mad Matt was murdered in cold blood, and his hideous ghost still waits down there for any souls who venture down, to be taken by him, screaming into the next world!"

"Really?" asked Jay.

"No." he grinned. "You're a real gullible kid, ain't you?" Jay felt his face reddening,

"Anyway," John went on, chuckling to himself, "I'm opening soon; I've got work to do. So off you two go, and try not to drown yourselves when the tide comes in!" He roared with laughter and went back into the Inn. Jay wasn't sure whether he was still joking or not.

The passageway was small and cramped. It was dug out from the solid rock, half by nature and half cut away by man. With Den leading by torchlight, Jay could barely see anything past Den's broad back as they travelled down in single file.

As the dim light of the cellar behind them faded away, they were locked into almost complete blackness, and it then became easy to imagine the dirty, rough smugglers making their way down to the sea, cursing at the slippery stones, and shivering in the dampness.

The boys made their way for ten minutes, banging their heads and scraping their arms, but still Den kept on laughing and joking all the way, and occasionally breaking out into a loud off-key version of Yo Ho Ho and a Bottle of Rum. Jay smiled, but he couldn't shake off the nagging fear that that remained in the back of his neck.

At last, and suddenly, they turned a bend and entered a small cave. The sea was very close outside, and the crashing water was loud and echoed in the hollow cavern.

"This is where Mad Matt Crowle was cruelly murdered!" Den announced dramatically. At once, the room seemed to swim around. Dizziness took hold of Jay and he felt himself fall to the ground.

"Hey Jay! What's up with you now man? You OK?"

Jay could faintly hear Den, but he was only aware that this was the cave of his nightmares, this was the spot where the huge body lay face down, and behind Den he could see the corner where the shadowy figure had been standing holding a knife.

A few moments later, he was feeling fine – and stupid – again! He decided to tell Den about the dreams, and the whole time he was telling his tale, Den sat listening with his mouth hanging open in astonishment.

"Wow!" Den exclaimed "Some story! It's like a ghost-murder mystery. Who killed Mad Matt? Where's the hidden treasure? Who screamed behind the locked door? Man this is great. We've gotta investigate. This is really cool!"

– Chapter 5 –

MAD UNCLE JOSS

Jay watched his excited friend with some amusement, but he was right, this was interesting, but also frightening. He and this boy were linked to a two hundred year old mystery, by blood and by murder. This whole thing may not turn out to be the fun adventure that Den seemed to be hoping for. Den wandered over to the corner where the shadowy figure had stood.

"Look!" he called "someone's carved stuff here. It could be a clue." Jay went over to look. There were carvings on the old walls, but mostly kids scratching rubbish and obscenities.

Den grinned, "I think he was murdered by Brittney who loves Martin." he laughed.

Jay said quietly "I think this is serious."

"But it's still fun though." Den grinned.

They walked out into the brilliant sunshine, and Jay was not surprised to see the same rugged beach from his dream. People had been screaming here. People had died.

Jay was staring out to sea thoughtfully, when a loud man's voice boomed out from above them,

"You! What you doing? I want you!" he was yelling from the top of the rocks above them.

"It's my Uncle Joss." Den shouted "he's as barmy as Mad Matt ever was, and twice as dangerous! Run! Get out of here!" And he turned to run back into the cave. Jay caught his arm,

"Wait a minute," Jay said "Is this another wind up?" but Den just flicked on the torch and raced back into the cave. Jay could hear the heavy footsteps of Joss almost to the entrance of the cave, and he decided not to hang about to find out – better to be laughed at than pulverised!

Den had taken off at such a speed, that Jay could barely see him ahead in the twisting tunnel. He scrambled after him – the heavy, clumsy boots of Mad Uncle Joss behind him sounding louder and closer by the second. As Den turned a corner up ahead, all light from the torch vanished with him, and Jay was plunged into total darkness.

Complete panic overtook him, and he crashed into a jutting out rock. He cut his forehead, stumbled to the ground seeing stars, and his legs just crumpled beneath him.

Joss had charged into the entrance of the tunnel behind them. He too was completely blind in the black caves.

"Come back you devils," he was roaring, "I know you've got it. It's mine and …." His shouting was cut short as his legs hit Jay on the ground and Joss came crashing down on top of him. At that moment, the cave lit up as Den came running back with the torch.

Like a terrified rabbit, Jay took advantage of the light and heaved himself free of the huge struggling man, and tore off down the passageway. Den took off after him, while Joss, still cursing loudly, tried to regain his footing on the slippery stone floor.

The boys burst back into the cellar like bats out of hell,

"Get your Dad!" Jay screamed, but Den shook his head and sat down,

"Joss will never follow us up here, he's too afraid of Dad." They both sat down on crates. Jay wiped a smear of blood from the cut in his forehead,

"What did he want?" Jay asked.

"Treasure" smiled Den, "He believes the old stories, that Wrecker Jack had a hidden fortune. The man's mad."

John appeared,

"Who's mad?" he asked "and what's happened to your head lad? You're a walking disaster you are!" He took a large cotton handkerchief from his pocket and shoved it roughly onto Jay's face.

"Uncle Joss is back," Den said, "He just chased us from the beach." John frowned,

"Just keep clear of him. I didn't know they'd let him out." He thought for a moment, "I'll give the prison a ring. You just stay away from him boys, d'ya hear?" The boys nodded.

When John left, Jay looked at Den for an explanation. Den leaned forward and whispered,

"He was put away for attacking three men in a bar – put all three of them in hospital!" Jay was impressed, Den went on,

"Not the first time either. He's got a violent temper and the strength of a bear. Mighty mean and plenty ugly." They laughed, but they also casually glanced back to the dark tunnel now and then just to make sure that Mad Uncle Joss didn't just turn up anyway.

– Chapter 6 –

ENCOUNTER ON THE MOORS

The boys wandered out to the moorland after lunch. They climbed the hilly Tors and rambled across the wild, desolated landscape until they were too tired to walk any further, and then they lay down and gazed at the clouds and sky. They talked for hours, about their families, their ambitions, girls, and how to find the missing treasure.

The contrast between the two boys was striking. Although both aged fourteen, Den was over 6ft tall, his ginger hair was shaven close to his head and his blue eyes could be both kind and menacing, depending upon his mood. He was thick built, heavy and strong, but deceptively agile when he needed to be.

Jay, on the other hand, was just under 6ft tall, lean, slim and athletic. Jay's hair was longer, and matched the colour of his dark hazel brown eyes. His jaw was strong and so was his character, and he carried a sense of right and wrong - he was interested in bravery and overcoming fear.

As they lay there on that hot sunny afternoon, alone in the middle of the moors, they could not know that more than two hundred years ago, two other lads had stopped in that exact spot when they were fourteen.

Linked by time and blood, Wrecker Jack and Mad Matt Crowle had lain there one sunny afternoon, before they became smugglers, before the killing and thieving entered their lives, and when they used to be good friends and good people.

"Why does your Uncle think we have the treasure?" Jay asked. Den laughed,

"Cos he's nuts."

"Apart from that?"

"Well, there was a lot of gold, rubies, emeralds, and stuff that Wrecker Jack and Mad Matt had between them, but after they were killed, none of it was ever found."

"So, why does he think *we* have it?"

"Cause he's nuts".

"Oh right." They laughed.

Something caught Jay's eye at the top of a far hill, something moved. He sat up and peered. Den sat up and saw the same thing – animal? Man?

"I hope that's not your crazy Uncle." Jay joked, but neither of them laughed.

The figure started to come towards them, slowly at first, but then running. A tall, clumsy man, running directly towards them, and then they both knew that crazy Uncle Joss was coming for them again.

"Shall we run?" Jay asked, he could see that Den was hesitating, as though he wanted to take his Uncle on. Den didn't reply.

"Your Dad told us to keep out of his way." Jay reminded him.

This seemed to have an impact on Den, he nodded, and then they turned and took off together, running back to the Inn.

The young boys easily outran the lumbering older man, and after a while they started to enjoy racing across the vast hilly open space. They ran fast and in step, like Olympic long distance runners, chasing a gold medal. They took a wrong turn, and despite Den being raised locally, it was very easy to mistake one craggy hill for another.

On and on they ran, breathless, laughing, until a root tugged at Jay's foot and he tripped at full speed, sending him flying into the air, before landing awkwardly at the foot of an old tree.

"Nice one!" Den laughed, coughing, trying to get his breath. Jay's only damage was a huge bruise to his ego, but he laughed anyway. Den slumped down next to him and looked around,

"We lost the old nutter." he grinned, but Jay still kept checking the landscape, just in case.

Jay's attention was drawn to the roots of an old tree, there was something familiar about it, but he couldn't quite work out what. He leaned over and peered into the gap between the roots and thought that he saw something catch the light.

He swept away the dead leaves and realised that there was something hidden there, old, metal, dirty, but again, it was really familiar. Reaching in he pulled out a large old belt buckle, and wiping away the dirt, he wondered if it might be silver.

"What's that?" Den asked, but before Jay could show him, a gravelly voice grunted,

"He died 'ere." They both quickly looked up, Uncle Joss was towering over them, but his eyes were fixed on the buckle.

"Who did?" Den asked, slightly less frightened than Jay.

"That pig, Wrecker Jack. There, when it were swamp, the dogs snappin' at 'im, them Excise men shoutin' at 'im, 'til he drowned in the wet mud".

Den was wondering if he could rush him, push him off balance. Jay was wondering if they could get away this time.

"Give it to me!" Joss demanded, his eyes fixed on the buckle.

Jay was considering whether to hand it over or not, when Den charged like a mad bull, his speed was incredible, and the force of his charge was awesome. He slammed into Joss's legs and sent the huge man flying backwards, landing with a massive crash into the bracken bushes.

"Run!" Den yelled, and Jay took off like a hare on a racing track. He could hear Den running behind him, and the roar of Joss's fury flying around the air.

They did outrun him in the end, and gasping, panting and bright red; they burst into the Inn like crazy chickens and lay down on the floor laughing. John was behind the bar cleaning glasses. He raised his eyebrows, shook his head, and threw down two bottles of water at them.

For ten minutes they lay there perfectly still getting their breath back.

"Hey, I know!" Den cried, suddenly jumping up (Jay just knew that he wasn't going to like the sound of this),

"Let's go see the witch!" he grinned.

Jay watched him hurry away; he shook his head and muttered to himself,

"A Witch - Really?"

– Chapter 7 –

MOTHER BLIGHT, WITCH OF THE MOORS

It was getting dark when they finally approached the old stone house. The warm orange sun was gently slipping behind ancient craggy hills. The loss of sunlight brought a cold shiver to the boys' bones.

"Tell me again why we're here?" Jay asked, whispering for no apparent reason,

"Tamson's family have been witches for centuries," Den explained, "We're going to show her the buckle. She might have a spell to find the treasure, or make Uncle Joss vanish, or something."

Jay shrugged his shoulders,

"Why not," he muttered, "after today, nothing would surprise me."

The ancient pathway led down a twisting slope. It was roughly made out of old rocks and stones, and crookedly took the visitors down to an ancient cottage, standing alone with a low thatch roof and small dark windows hewn out of a dirty white wall. Visitors were led to the splintered wooden door, and the heavy rusty iron knocker.

Jay reached out to lift the heavy knocker, but before he had the chance to lift it, a voice screeched at him,

"Don't you go knocking on my door!"

They both jumped back and waited. Silence. They looked at each other and grinned, and then the voice came back even louder,

"Well, come in if you're going to, otherwise, go away!"

Jay pushed the door handle, and the door slowly swung open with a predictably weird creaking sound. They resisted the temptation to laugh. The formidable looking old woman in front of the fire however, was nothing to smile about.

The cottage consisted of one wide, dark room. It was smoke filled from the open burning fireplace, and smelt of damp and animals. It was like the movie set of a witch's coven, with black, low wooden beams adorned with dead birds and rabbits, and then shelves and shelves of strange bottles, books and boxes.

The huddled old witch was wearing a long black dress with a black shawl around her shoulders. She sat deathly still before the crackling fire, smoking a long, thin clay pipe.

"So?" She said abruptly – suddenly staring at them, her eyes were bright green, her face wise and knowing, not kind, not unkind, just strong and clever. It was hard to say how old she was, the white hair and the way she dressed suggested ancient, but she was probably younger than she appeared.

"Can we come in?" Jay asked politely, as they hovered in the doorway.

"You *are* in." she grunted, drawing on the clay pipe, and turning her face back to the fire,

"And if that's all you want, then you're easily settled!"

The boys looked at each other, still suppressing almost overwhelming impulses to burst out laughing, and crack jokes about black cats and toads.

They waited, and she ignored them. The fire crackled and spat quietly, and as their eyes adjusted to the dark room, they could make out an old bed in the far corner, strange dusty ornaments and dirty brown walls, coloured by the smoking fire over hundreds of years.

They quietly walked over to the huge fireplace and stood nervously by the woman. Her hair was long and white, her profile quite frightening. Eventually she slowly turned her head and looked up at Den.

"Den." She said, as a way of greeting to the taller lad.

"Mother Blight." He replied seriously. Then she looked at Jay. He looked back, they stared into each other's eyes for a moment, and then she nodded,

"Wrecker Jack's spawn!" she growled and spat into the fire. Den started to smile, Jay sighed, he was getting used to this by now. After a short silence, she looked sharply back at him,

"What d'you want?" she growled. Jay held out the buckle to her, it shone in the firelight. She looked at it intently, slowly placed the clay pipe in the fireplace and stood up. She was tall and looked down on Jay.

"Is it real?" she asked,

"I think so," said Jay, "we found it on the moors, half buried, near an old tree." She ignored Jay and looked at Den, he nodded, and her bright eyes turned back to the old belt buckle gleaming in the fire glow. She took the buckle and cupped in her hands and closed her eyes.

"Bad magic" she whispered, "powerful danger, you must leave this place boy," she opened her eyes wide and stared at Jay and then screamed,

"NOW!"

Jay backed up a few paces,

"Why?" he asked in terror, she paused, and then said quietly,

"Because it's tea time." She turned and walked away to the darkest corner of the room. Jay turned to Den.

"What?"

– Chapter 8 –

THE WITCH'S ADVICE

Den was smiling and shaking his head,

"She's winding you up." He laughed. Jay turned to Mother Blight who had swiftly changed clothes behind an old curtain, and was now wearing jeans, sweatshirt and trainers. Her wild mane of hair was neatly tied up into a ponytail and she was holding a carrier bag and laughing.

"Sorry," she laughed, "couldn't resist. It's just my act for the tourists; they pay good money for their fortunes told and this performance."

"So, you're not a real witch then?" Jay asked, his pounding heart finally beginning to calm down,

"Oh, I didn't say that now." She replied, "I can still be a witch with all the powers of my ancestors, but that doesn't mean that I can't have central heating and satellite television. This is just my place of work, come on, I'll show you where I live, my real witches coven."

Den was still chuckling as they all bundled out of the small cottage, after Mother Blight had put out the fire (which turned out to be gas fired), and locked up the old place using several security locks and a burglar alarm.

It was icy cold outside as the wind off the moors whipped through the night, chilling their bodies through to the bone. Jay hoped that they didn't have to walk far. He might have guessed that around the back of the cottage there would be parked out of site, an impressive black Range Rover. Jay was glad, he thought he would be better off in the warm, leather-bound interior – but that was before he sampled Mother Blight's driving!

It only took ten swift, blood-curdling minutes for them to arrive at Mother Blight's house. She lived in a comfortable but small, terraced house in the nearby town looking out to sea. It was warm and friendly, and inhabited (predictably) by many black cats that had the run of the house. She called out to her daughter to make tea, but frowned when she realised that she was out on the town again.

After Mother Blight had made sandwiches for them all, the boys told her about their adventures, and she listened without saying a word. Two cats purred on her lap as she stroked them in silence.

The boys hungrily devoured sandwiches as they waited for her to speak – each with a black cat sitting on the back of the sofa curled around the back of their heads.

"What do you want from me?" she finally asked, looking at Jay, but Jay didn't know. Den answered instead,

"We wondered if there was something you could do, to control the dreams. You know, to let Jay stay in the dream a bit longer to find out what happened."

"Why?" she asked. They didn't have a good answer to that, apart from curiosity. They both shrugged. Mother Blight took the belt buckle from Jay's hand.

She looked at Jay and said,

"Were you the first person to touch this buckle since it was put there by Wrecker Jack?" He nodded, he assumed so. "And you are a direct blood relative of Jack Pengelli?" He nodded again.

"Then it may work. This is the key" she said looking at the buckle, "but you don't realise how dangerous this can be." She looked at the boys, but she could see only two boys on an exciting adventure, who would not listen to caution, and who would not care about danger.

"If you use this key to go into a dream, then you will be in the dream." she explained. They shrugged,

"No you don't understand," she went on "When you wake up everything will be back the way it was, you cannot change anything by being in the dream, so even if you blow up the whole village, when you wake up it will be back as it was. But, you can be changed."

The boys looked at each other blankly. She sighed,

"You will be so completely a part of the dream, that if you are hurt or killed in the dream, then your body will really feel it – if you die in the dream, then you really die."

"Cool." said Den. Jay wasn't quite so excited by this news.

"Alright then," she said, "I will make a herb potion, which may or may not work, and you will place the herbs under your pillow at night with this buckle." the boys were both grinning. "I will also give you a crystal – smash the crystal when you want to wake up."

She sighed, and went out into a small back room full of bottles, herbs and plants, and rows upon rows of shelves full of flowerpots, brimming with leaves and flowers, rich strange aromas, all potent with natural magic.

She shook her head; there was no way that this was going to end well.

– Chapter 9 –

INTO THE DREAM

Jay's problem that night was that he was too excited to sleep! It was two o'clock in the morning, he had the herbs and buckle under his pillow, and he was wide-awake. Den, on the other hand, who had stayed the night to give support, was snoring loudly on the floor.

Jay lay back on the (lumpy) pillow and closed his eyes; he began to imagine the beach, the waves from outside his room providing the background sounds, and his head provided the screams and terror, and then suddenly, like a train rushing through a tunnel, he was hurled into the dream, landing violently on the hard stone beach – into the storm and into the nightmare…

Darkness engulfed him; shadows of screaming people raced past him and the rain lashed his face. He looked at his arm, it was bleeding painfully, and he realised what Mother Blight had been warning him about – this was real, he could be hurt now, and he could die.

Jay was wet and shivering. This time he knew that he was in a dream, and he knew that he had to get to the cave to solve his mystery, but this time, he was really terrified. The entrance to the cave was very near, and he could see flickering candlelight and two huge men fighting.

As Jay approached the cave he saw one of the men stab the other with a long, wide knife. There was a cry and the man fell to the ground. Jay ran towards the entrance but was unable to stay out of sight as he skidded on the pebbles and fell at the feet of the man with the bloody knife. Jay looked up into the murderous eyes of Wrecker Jack.

"Come 'ere!" he growled at Jay. A noise behind Jack made him turn as a shadowy figure hidden there moved. Jay took his chance and ran passed Jack and into the black caves behind him.

This time there was no torchlight to guide him, and no Den to save him. Jay had to feel his way desperately in the pitch-black tunnel as fast as he could, with the screams from the beach and the heavy boots of Jack echoing all around him.

It took fifteen exhausting minutes to reach the end of the tunnel into the cave at the back of the Inn. Jay emerged cut and bleeding, his heart drumming in his ears, his eyes sore with salt water. In terror he stumbled in the dark to the oak door to the Inn and banged on it for help.

He screamed for help but no one heard him – and at the back of his mind he knew that this is the moment that he had lived before, but this time he was in the past, this time Den's Dad was not there to open the door and save him.

Wrecker Jack burst into the small cellar with a roar of fury and stood in the entrance trying to adjust his eyes to the dark room. Jay fell silent. His only way out was through the other cave tunnel, the one leading to Mad Matt's house. Jay crouched down behind a barrel and watched Jack silently.

He could see the outline of a giant of a man, well over six foot tall and wide as a house. He was dressed in dirty black clothes, with matted black hair and beard, big black mud spattered boots and

black evil eyes that shone even in the darkness. 'I'm related to that.'
He thought.

Back in Jay's bedroom, Den was wakened by Jay screaming for help in his sleep. Jay stopped calling, but was still tossing and turning, he looked scared. Den started to panic, he shook Jay but the deep sleep could not be stopped. As the covers slipped away from Jay, Den's heart missed a beat when he saw that Jay was sweating and in distress. Den grabbed the pillow, snatched up the buckle and the herbs, and threw them across the room. Jay awoke.

Jay drank two glasses of water before he could stop shaking and speak.

"So?" asked Den, "What happened?"

"It was Wrecker Jack"

"What was?"

"It was Wrecker Jack who killed the man in the cave". Den nodded "we already know that, but where's the hidden treasure?" Den asked. Jay shrugged his shoulders.

They both sat silently for a while.

"Are you going back?" Den asked. Jay didn't answer.

– Chapter 10 –

THE SQUIRE WAS ANGRY

(Back in the past - February 1790)

The Squire of the Manor house was a powerful and dangerous man. He ran half the businesses in the County, and he also organised smuggling and crime on a large scale, with many of the local Excise men working for him.

He was tall with square shoulders, and a large square face. Thick bushy eyebrows hung over a pair of piercing blue eyes, a hooked nose and a mouth that seldom turned up unless profit was involved. He took great strides when walking, arms swinging energetically at his sides as though marching, and he was tremendously strong.

On the night of the storm, Squire Dawkins had been waiting for his men to return from a smuggling voyage with a boat laden with silks, rum and other treasure. But the hours had passed by and he was becoming impatient and angry. The huge door suddenly slammed back and it echoed through the high wooden hall. Three wet, bedraggled men ran in.

"Where's my gold?!" the Squire roared, slamming a solid silver tankard down onto the heavy oak table "and where's my daughter?!"

The three men stopped – the Squire had men put to death for far less.

"Well?" he demanded turning red-faced with fury. One of the men stepped forward,

"The ship was wrecked in the storm Squire," one man replied shakily "Jack and Mad Matt were there with their men – but it all went bad."

"AND?" he bellowed,

"It shed its cargo; we couldn't stop the villagers from pillaging any that come ashore." The Squire slowly stood up glaring down at the rain soaked man,

The Squire grabbed up the tankard and hurled it at the man who ducked as the heavy missile flew past his ear, splashing red wine over the polished wooden floor.

"Squire!" he pleaded "Jack knifed Mad Matt, and the Excise men took after Jack across the moors with dogs, and Jack sank into the mud and he's dead an' all"

"And where's my treasure?" the square spat between clenched teeth, but he knew the answer – it was gone – there was a traitor in his house.

The Squire was about to start ordering hangings when a flustered serving girl came rushing into the hall, crying and in a great panic.

"What's this?" the Squire turned his anger to the girl. The girl, distressed and terrified, spoke quickly and fearfully to the huge, angry man,

"Squire, Squire," she gasped, "Miss Genefer has run away with her jewels, she's gone to Liskeard on the pony trap, to catch the coach to Plymouth. I couldn't stop her, I tried, really I did.

The men all stepped away from the girl who threw herself sobbing onto the floor. There was silence. The Squire's face became redder, his eyes bulging in his head – they thought his head would explode.

The girl stayed still on the floor; she looked like a prisoner awaiting execution. Then, as though defeated, the Squire just sat down and stared at the table. No one dared to move, the Squire was thinking – never the time to disturb a dangerous man.

– Chapter 11 –

BACK INTO THE DREAM

Den could not talk him out of it. Jay was convinced that he could sneak back, this time without being seen by Wrecker Jack, that he could find out more; maybe even find the hiding place of the missing gold. Besides, they now knew that he could be brought back from the dream if the items were removed from under his pillow (probably).

Jay's four year old sister Katie, however, was proving to be a problem. His mum had gone away to stay with an elderly aunt for the night, and left Katie with him. Den liked this less and less. As night fell, Jay put Katie to bed. She was surprised at the attention, bedtime stories and milky drinks, and soon fell peacefully asleep in the early evening.

Jay felt strangely fond of Katie that night as she lay quietly sleeping, cuddling her teddy, with her long lashes tightly closed and her small mouth slightly smiling. He was worried that he may not wake up from his sleep that night, but he was set on finding the treasure in the past, somehow claiming it in the present, and so taking away all his family's financial problems.

Den was determined to stay awake this time. Jay struggled to sleep, and once again he was unable to sleep until 2am.

Den awoke with a start. It was dark, he had fallen asleep again and he could have kicked himself. Something was wrong. The bedroom door was now open; it was shut when he lay down. He jumped up and looked at Jay, he was still there sleeping, but his face was sweating and he was frowning and restless. But what Den saw next turned his heart to ice.

Katie had awoken in the night and had climbed into bed with her brother – her little head was lying on the pillow, and she too could have been thrown into the nightmare world? But when had she climbed in? Jay must have already been asleep or he would not have let her – that meant that she had arrived later, that he didn't even know that she was there.

Mother Blight was awakened by the sound of her telephone. Squinting at her clock she saw it was the middle of the night, and she had a bad feeling about the call.

"Mother Blight!" Den yelled, "Jay's gone into the dream and his little sister was sleeping next to him and so does this mean that she's gone into the dream with him? And then if so, Jay doesn't know that she's there! What do I do?"

"What? How old is she?"

"Only four. She must have climbed into his bed when I was asleep"

"What were you doing sleeping?" Tamson Blight demanded,

"Can I wake them up? Shall I take out the stuff from the under the pillow?"

"No, you can't do that." She said angrily, "The link is from the buckle and Jay. If his sister has joined him in the dream, then it is because she shared his pillow, which means that she can only get back if she is with him."

"What can I do?"

"Only two things."

"Yes?"

"Wait and hope that they find each other before Jay wakes up"

"Or?"

"Or, go to sleep on the same pillow and try to find them"

"What happens if Jay wakes up before he finds Katie?"

"I don't know. She may wake up, or she may never wake up. I don't know."

"Help me Mother Blight. Help me to go to sleep."

Mother Blight drove to the house at law-breaking speed. Den was on the doorstep waiting. They ran upstairs, and then Den gently pushed the sleeping brother and sister over so that he could squeeze onto the edge of the pillow.

Jay swallowed the draft that Mother Blight handed him, then almost immediately, his mind was gone from the present and dragged mercilessly into the past.

Chapter 12

DEN GOES INTO THE DREAM

Den had heard Jay describe the dream to him, but nothing prepared him for the noise and cold and terror of that storm-drenched beach that night.

A half-submerged ship was being tossed about in the savage black sea water, and the waves were washing over screaming people and dead bodies. The shore was crawling with people surviving or looting, and the shouting and screaming on the shore told him that lives were being taken as well as goods.

He looked desperately around for Katie, but everything and everyone looked like the same black shadowy figures, and when he shouted, his words were snatched from his mouth by the howling wind and stolen away into the night. The small cave was nearby, and so he started to go towards the entrance, calling all the time for Katie.

Den's tall and muscular build meant that he was not approached by anyone. He had rage building inside him, and where Jay's fear had grown with every step, Den had only anger, building into fury with every step. He was mad at Jay for being so stupid, he was mad at Katie for being in danger, he was mad at Mother Blight for giving them the herbs, but most of all, the biggest rage of all, was for himself for falling asleep and not protecting his friend and little sister.

Den stormed into the cave and almost fell over the dead body on the ground. Unceremoniously Den rolled him over with his foot.

"Well, well, Mad Uncle Matt, we meet at last." he muttered. Den looked into the shadows; Jay and Wrecker Jack were gone.

Den was surprised to find his torch still in his pocket; he flicked it on, and started off determinedly down the dark, stone passageway. He met no one, and no one chased him. At the end of the tunnel he found an empty room. He tried the oak door and found it was locked, turning he started off without hesitation down the other passageway towards Mad Matt's house.

As he hurried down the passageway he tried to remember everything that had already happened, one fact he did know for sure was that Excise Men had chased Wrecker Jack across the moors with dogs, and he died in the marshes.

Assuming (hopefully) that they were unable to change the future from within a dream, that must be where Jack is now, and perhaps Jay is with him. He tried not to even think about Katie, as that just put a crushing cold grip around his heart and stopped him from thinking clearly.

The tunnel ended in the basement of Mad Matt's dark house. It was deserted, but there were signs of a struggle. Tables and chairs were turned over, and the back door was wide open and banging in the howling gale. Without missing a step, Den strode out of the house and found that he was facing the wilderness of the Cornish moors.

His torch made no impact on the absolute blackness of the moors at night, so he turned it off to save the batteries. The land was bare, muddy, and full of sharp bracken and barren trees. It was dangerous during the day and absolutely treacherous at night.

There was a distant and faint howling of dogs to the right of him, and so Den headed that way. The icy winds stung his face and blinded his eyes, but nothing was going to stop him. He hurried as fast as he could, fighting the elements, he rushed towards the baying dogs, hoping that they would lead him to Jack and Jay.

The sound of the dogs gradually grew louder, until he could finally also hear the voices of the Excise Men shouting to each other across the moors. Still he gained ground, until finally he could see the tiny flickering lamps that the Excise men were carrying in their pursuit.

– Chapter 13 –

JAY AND JACK

Suddenly, a faint call drew Den's attention. It sounded like Jay, but it was to his left and away from the search party, and yet Den was sure it was him. Taking a chance he changed direction and made his way towards where he thought he had heard him.

Taking care to keep to high ground, Den knew enough about the moors to avoid low, flat areas that could contain soft, wet marshland - strong enough to suck a man down like sticky toffee and drown him in mud in minutes.

Den was relieved to find that he had made the right decision, as in the dim light; he saw the outline of Jay running across the moors chasing someone.

Wrecker Jack was running for his life. He knew the hounds would soon pick up his scent, but he wasn't going to give up lightly. He cursed himself for not telling his wife where his fortune was hidden, and just hoped that he could get away long enough to get to her. He had told her where he kept the only clue, but now it looked like he was going to take that to his grave.

Jack was keenly aware of his surroundings, and quickly sensed that a lone person was following him across the moors. He knew it wasn't Matt, because he had made sure that he was dead – why should he have to share all his fortune with that imbecile – that traitor? Matt was just muscle; it was well known that Jack was the brains, and that even the Squire was scared of him.

Jack hid behind a wide tree to see who was behind him, and was amused to see a slim, young boy chasing clumsily through the mud and bracken. The glint of the dagger in Jack's hand caught the light of the moon as it peeped through the storm clouds for a moment. Jay stopped dead a few yards from the tree; he sensed that there was a shadow, a thing or a person there.

Jay remained absolutely still, straining to see through the darkness, barely breathing he waited. Then out from the blackness stepped a mountain of a man, eyes like coal, face of evil, with the dirt from the moors streaked across his face like some ancient primitive warrior.

Jay was horrified that some of the features were so like his Dad's – the nose, the shape of the face but not the character, not the heart of stone.

They stood absolutely still looking at each other, Jack casually turning the bloodied knife around in his hand as though deciding whether to attack or laugh at this boy who had the nerve to chase him.

"Who are 'ee boy?" he demanded at last, the wind stirring around them, and the sinister outline of the smuggler towering over him.

Jay didn't answer, what could he say? He was very aware of the knife, and also of the power of this man. He knew that he was faster, more agile, but he realised that if Jack was able to get close enough, then he would not be able to fight him off.

Jay couldn't help staring at the shiny belt buckle around the broad smugglers coat; it was the same one that he had found all those centuries later.

"State your business or I'll send 'ee to hell!" Wrecker Jack demanded.

"I'm family." Jay said, "I'm a Pengelli." The smuggler was confused, he looked the boy up and down and then laughed out loud.

"Crazy is what 'ee are!" he growled and lunged suddenly at him with the knife. Jay was expecting the attack and easily jumped out of his way. Jack lunged with such ferocity that he could not stop and stumbled into bracken which tore at his clothes and face. He roared with anger.

The course dry grass underfoot was noisy; it was pointless trying to hide. The hounds were still barking in the distance and the voices of the excise men were faint but clear – they were hunting Jack and they intended to kill him on sight.

"Who are 'ee?" Jack growled again, moving gradually towards Jay "What dya want?"

Jay squared up to him and looked him in his black empty eyes and said,

"Jay Pengelli." Jack hesitated, looked again at the boy.

"Yee're no Pengelli that I've ever met" he growled, "Skinny, strange boy, no, not of my blood, but I will spill some of yee'rs just to see what colour it comes out." and he threw back his head and laughed.

Jay took his chance and grabbed Jack's wrist to try to wrestle away the knife. Jack was even stronger than he looked, and with a sweep of his arm Jay was thrown across the ground.

Hearing Jack running at him, Jay rolled over to avoid the knife that was then thrust into the ground inches from where his head had been a moment ago.

Jay jumped to his feet and cried out:

"Stop! Don't do this!"

Jack smiled with his rotten teeth, but not with his eyes. Then he slowly reached into the pocket of his great coat and pulled out a pistol.

– Chapter 14 –

WORD OF HONOUR

Jay froze. He desperately looked around for somewhere to hide, but the ground was flat, and the clumps of bracken were sharp and sparse. Jack cocked the pistol, still smiling, still locked eye to eye with Jay.

The boy was shaking; he was covered in mud, scared, but still not begging for his life. Jack liked this, he was going to kill him anyway, but still it was good to die a man's death and not like all the other miserable souls who had snivelled and cried at the end of their days.

Jack smiled and pulled the trigger, Jay flinched, but the gun jammed. As Jack tried to reload, Jay took off running like a hare. Jack roared in anger and lumbered after him in fury, but with this roar the hounds were back on his trail and heading straight for them.

Jay scrambled to hide behind a grey granite rock and in the pitch-black night, Jack lost sight of him, but still he rushed on, he was not to be insulted or outwitted by a boy.

Then Jack felt the ground move, the soft ground turned to oozing mud and water, and terror gripped the smugglers heart as he realised that the moor had got him and he would be pulled down into the bog.

He struggled to get free, but that only increased the speed of his descent, the gluey brown mud sucked him down and he knew he would not be able to pull himself from this. Fury was in his eyes as he roared and battled to get free.

Jay watched as Jack sank to his waist, he had dropped his pistol into the mud and was now thrashing about like a trapped wild animal. Jay stepped out from behind the rock.

"Jack!" he called out "If you give me your word not to harm me, I'll pull you free".

"Get me out lad, I'm drownin'!" he called back.

"Give me your word!" Jay demanded,

"You have my oath lad, on the heads of my wife and cheeld, pull me free lad."

Jay couldn't find any branches or anything long enough to reach him.

"Throw me one end of your belt," He called out, taking care not to go too near to the edge of the soft mud.

Jack struggled to pull off his heavy belt, but managed it finally, and threw one end across to Jay as the mud rose to his chest.

"Pull me out quick, I'll not hurt ee now lad, you've my word of honour!"

The hounds and excise men sounded close now, but it was too dark to see where they were.

The end of the belt splattered on the ground at Jay's feet, with the heavy buckle sinking in the middle.

Jay started to pull, but Jack was dead weight and the bog was pulling him down. Jay pulled until the rough leather belt cut into his hands but still he would not let go. Then bit by bit the huge dark man emerged from beneath the liquid ground and crawled out by Jay's feet, exhausted, soaked, and covered in wet mud like an oozing creature.

Jay sat near to him, he was out of breath and his hands were bleeding. Then from the corner of his eye he caught a glimpse of metal, and suddenly Jack had him by the throat with the knife pressed against his neck.

He smelt of rotting leaves, mud, rum and wet leather.

"You gave me your word of honour." Jay managed to whisper,

"Ain't got no honour lad" he whispered close to his face, then laughed.

– Chapter 15 –

THE EXCISE MEN

Jay closed his eyes and waited. He expected to die then.

There was a thud and a shudder and then Jack let go. Jay threw himself away from the knife and saw that someone had hit Jack over the head, making him fall back into the quicksand.

"Come on!" someone urgently whispered pulling Jays arm. He looked up but could not understand how Den was there. He was dazed and confused, and then the excise men and dogs burst through the darkness. Den dragged Jay back behind the granite rocks as the excise men surrounded Jack.

"Help me!" Jack was screaming, now terrified to be back in the same peril. The dogs were barking at him as he floundered and shouted in the wet mud. The excise men were just standing there talking amongst themselves.

"Come on." whispered Den urgently, trying to drag Jay away "we have to go!"

"No, the belt buckle is there and Jack."

"Doesn't matter" said Den "Katie is here."

"What?" Jay said confused, "No she's not."

"She was asleep on your pillow; Mother Blight says that puts her with you in this dream."

"Where?"

"Don't know, I don't even know when she arrived, Jay I can't find her."

"What!" Jay froze, his senses, his mind, he could not take in this information, this nightmare.

He followed Den as they turned to go back to the shore. Jack was still shouting, and begging for help, but as they left, they heard one excise man say,

"Leave him be, let the moors take him, it will save us the trouble of hangin' him".

– Chapter 16 –

WHERE IS KATIE?

The boys arrived back at the beach as daybreak was starting. The storm had subsided, and the cruel sea was now calm and gentle. The bright new sun was silently rising over the sea, as the boys sat down wearily upon the stone beach and watched the sky slipping into different colours.

Jay was too exhausted and desperate to speak, there was no sign of Katie, and the seashore was littered with broken wood, torn clothes and blood. There was very little hope that she could have survived alone out there, so there were two options, the first was that someone had taken her away, and the second was that she had been killed in the chaos of the night before, and removed or washed out to sea. Both options were unthinkable.

They were dirty, wet, cold and tired. Den stood up, and Jay followed in silence. They wearily walked off the beach and towards the small nearby row of fishermen's cottages. The streets were mainly deserted, but there were a few fishermen preparing to go to sea.

Jay was beyond fear now, he couldn't find his sister, and to make it worse, he could sense that Den was on the verge of a complete meltdown, and he didn't know what his incredibly strong new friend would be capable of if he lost control.

The cold morning light put down a spotlight onto the stricken ship. It lay in three main pieces, black and torn like a scorched tree that had been ripped apart by a bolt of lightning. The shore was littered with shattered wooden planks, torn clothes and smashed vases and bottles. Seagulls screamed and circled and swarmed, but the boys did not want see what they were swarming over.

The good people of the town had removed the bodies and the booty - they had saved all the souls they could, and then they set about saving their own hungry families by taking whatever they could find from the ship wreck.

It was not clear whether this was a genuine tragedy, or whether the wreckers had deliberately signalled the ship onto the rocks to be destroyed and plundered. Either way, it was a desolate and terrible place that morning.

An old lady passed by and asked them if they were looking for the dead. When they nodded, she pointed to a row of sheds at the end of the lane where the pilchards were cleaned and stored in salt. Jay closed his eyes for a moment; Den put a hand on his shoulder and said,

"Let me go, it's my fault." Jay looked at him for a moment; there was the same pain in Dens eyes as his own.

"No," he said, "My sister, my fault."

They walked together towards the pilchard sheds, wanting to rush to find out, but at the same time wanting to go slowly to not find out.

As they approached the building, the strong distinct smell of fish hit them, and the air was filled with the sound of crying – not wailing or huge outpouring of grief, but quiet, sad, weeping.

They entered the long dark building. In the far corner a huddle of people were gathered around a line of about thirty bodies covered in rough oilcloths. Jay stood back and looked at the covered bodies - only a few would be local, lost in the battle of the night before, most would be unknown sailors and travellers from the ship.

Jay could not move. Den walked quickly along the line of covered bodies without hesitating from one end to the other and without uncovering any of them. Jay watched him in silence. Then he came back to Jay,

"She's not here." he said quietly.

"How do you know? You didn't look at any of them?"

"They are all grown-ups," Den said, "she was only little, there are no children here."

Chapter 17

KATIE IS STILL LOST

It took a full minute for this to sink in, and then Jay realised that he had been holding his breath for quite a while, and now, for a moment, he could breathe again.

The smell of the fish was overpowering. They left the shed and walked away to the far end of the old stone pier and looked around. There were around four excise men standing at one end of the beach, but they did not seem to be very interested, and in fact they all appeared to be drunk.

"Are you sure that bad stuff can really happen to us in this dream?" Jay said.

Den shrugged, "Mother Blight didn't know."

They heard someone shout out "Tynners are coming" – this seemed to have an immediately sobering effect on the excise men, who looked around, suddenly startled and agitated.

The boys watched with detached interest as the excise men quickly scurried away as the beach was invaded by hundreds of men from the tin mines carrying axes. They descended upon the shore like a giant swarm of ants, clearing everything they found on the beach, and then wading out to sea to the stricken ship.

Like a menacing dark cloud, they hacked at the ship, removing the timber, ropes, masts and everything attached and took it away. They seemed to have no end to them, and Jay was sure that more than a thousand men were now on the small stony beach stripping the vessel bare and removing it onto pony carts waiting in the cobbled streets nearby.

The boys turned away, it meant nothing to them. They started to walk aimlessly, looking, listening, and trying to find a clue, an idea, something that would lead them to Katie.

They walked past the small Fishermen's cottages and as they approached a battered cottage door, Jay stopped dead. Then Den saw it too. A little piece of yellow material, tied to a door handle - material with a pattern on it, material not available in those days and looking remarkably like the nightdress that Katie had been wearing.

They stood before the peeling wooden green door and Jay gently removed the piece of material. He angrily wiped away a rogue tear in his eye and knocked on the door, he had a terrible feeling about what he was going to find inside.

After a while they heard someone move about inside, then a girls voice called out,

"Who's there?" Jay replied,

"I'm Jay; I'm looking for my sister Katie." There was no answer,

"She is only four; a piece of her nightie is tied to your door." Still no answer.

"Please," he begged, "Please, I must find her."

Then there was the sound of a bolt being pulled back, and the door slowly opened a crack, and they could see a scared face peering at them from inside the dark house. Den wanted to kick the door in, but Jay saw him move to kick it in and he pushed in front to block him.

"Is Katie here?" Jay asked gently again. After a moment, the door opened wider, and they saw a young girl standing there. She looked about sixteen, very pretty, with long curly auburn hair, and beautiful white skin and green eyes. The boys waited, they didn't want to frighten her any more.

The girl was dressed in fine blue cloth, but the dress was muddy and ripped. The girl opened the door wide, and allowed them to pass her and to go into the small, candle lit house. Den thought he knew her from somewhere? In the far corner a warm fire was burning and crackling in the grate, and by the flames they could make out the figure of a small child lying perfectly still on her back on the top of a wooden bench.

It reminded them of the bodies in the pilchard shed, covered with the rough blankets all in a row. Her head and body were covered with a blanket, but the small dirty feet of a child were peeping out at the end.

Jay stood in the doorway, his feet on cold uneven stones looking across at the figure lying still on the long bench. A shudder ran through him like an earthquake. Anger and sadness broke his heart.

"Oh no." whispered Den - the words were hardly audible.

"Katie!" Jay shouted out in despair, but then a soft hand rested on his arm.

"No," whispered the girl. He looked into her eyes; the candlelight was dancing there,

"No," she said again quietly "the child could not sleep with the light of the candles in her eyes so she pulled the .."

But he didn't wait to hear the end, without knowing how, he was on the floor by the bench and he had pulled back the cover. Katie was sleeping – dirty face, hair knotted with salt water, but alive and sleeping.

Jay felt as though a heavy black weight lifted from his soul and released him. He became aware of a shawl being placed about his shoulders, and only then did he realise that he was shuddering with cold and damp, and he allowed the girl to guide him to a large battered old chair near to the fire.

Den sank down exhausted on a nearby wooden bench, and warmed his hands by the glowing fire.

The girl put a piece of wood on the fire, and then handed the boys a cup of brandy and water.

"Where did you find her?" Den asked the girl.

"She was just on the beach, by the cave. It wasn't safe, I brought her home." She spoke quietly, and looked at the floor as she spoke. Jay looked at her,

"Thank you." he said. She nodded, and looked back into the fire.

"Jay?" moaned Katie, stirring and now turning towards him sleepily.

Jay went to her and kneeled at her side,

"I couldn't find you," she said complaining sleepily, but he just hugged her until she squirmed and moaned about being squeezed too tight.

"Can we go home now?" Katie yawned, Jay nodded. The two boys thanked the girl again, and led Katie out into the street. Den looked around to make sure that no-one was near, and then he smashed the witch's crystal onto the cobbled stones.

Almost immediately, they were back in the bedroom, in the present, in a big huddle in the middle of a small single bed, and looking up at a very angry witch.

– Chapter 18 –

SITTING ON THE BAY

Den and Jay sat on the low stone wall which encircled the harbour, hanging their feet over the edge. Mother Blight had let them know in no uncertain terms that she was furious, and that they were not to bother her ever again.

The sky was a hundred different shades of light blue, with scatterings of soft white clouds and a warm orange sun. The sea was dressed to match the sky, and it too was a beautiful array of pale blue, pale green and turquoise, broken neatly at the edges by a dainty white spray.

A noisy, bustling day, with tourists and children making noise and chaos, intervened with the gentle lapping of the sea on the rocks and the crying seagulls circling for someone to throw them chips.

Den was staring at the sea and Jay was turning the belt buckle over and over in his hands.

"Well," said Den finally, "Did you find any clues?"

Jay shook his head and sighed. He had hoped to find something on the buckle that would give him some idea of where to look; he just had the feeling that the buckle held a clue. No inscriptions, no drawings, no scratches, nothing. His Mum would be back in a couple of days from moving his Dad from the hospital in London to a one nearby, and he had achieved nothing – apart from nearly killing his own sister.

Den took the heavy buckle off him.

"Heavy." he said turning it over, "Thick."

Jay looked at him,

"Thick?" he repeated,

Then, they both had the same idea at the same time. Jay tried to snatch it back, but Den held it out of reach.

"My idea." he said laughing, and took out his penknife. Jay held his breath as he watched Den trying to pry the brass buckle in two, at first nothing, but then a crack appeared and with a twist, the buckle fell into two pieces, and a small piece of old parchment fell out.

Jay carefully opened the delicate note and they both read the scrawling writing inside.

'Wife, look in mirrer'

"I don't think there _is_ a mirror at the pub" Den said thoughtfully, squinting his eyes as he tried to remember.

"Old Jack had good handwriting for an ugly bloke," smiled Jay, "Rubbish at spelling though."

They stood up and brushed away the sand on their jeans and set off for the pub without another word between them. It was early, and the lunchtime trade at the Inn hadn't started yet. John Crowle was drying glasses behind the bar.

"Now what you two up to then?" he asked as the boys walked in looking suspicious.

"Nothing." said Den. Jay just shrugged.

"Well as long as you do it quietly." John muttered, chuckling at his own humour.

The boys wandered around looking at all the walls but no mirror. Jay looked at the large painting of Wrecker Jack over the fireplace. John watched them.

"Was this painting always there?" Jay asked casually,

John thought for a minute then said,

"No, that's only been there about thirty years."

The boys looked at each other,

"So," continued Jay casually, "what was there before?"

"I dunno," his dad replied "What d'you want to know for?" They both shrugged their shoulders again. John sighed.

"Well, if you really care, there's an old photo book out back in the office. Pictures were taken about a hundred years ago, might be a picture of the bar in there." They hurried out and John shook his head,

"Trouble," he muttered, "I smell trouble."

– Chapter 19 –

THE OLD MIRROR

In the back office, Den found a large scruffy leather-bound book on the top of a filing cabinet. After looking through for a while they found what they were looking for – a sepia photograph of the old fireplace and sure enough, hanging above it was a large plain mirror.

The boys took the album out to John and showed him the photo. He glanced at it and then carried on putting the glasses away.

"It's a mirror." said Jay.

"Well done." said John.

"I don't suppose you know where it is?" asked Den casually,

John put down his dishcloth,

"Now why d'you want to know about an old mirror for?" he asked.

"History project." said Den quickly.

"Yeah right." John replied. They waited. Finally he sighed and said,

"It might be out in the back of the cellar, but it's most likely to be smashed after all this time". The boys tried not to look excited and strolled over to the cellar door, then both rushed to get through first. John watched them and slowly shook his head,

"Weird." he muttered.

Den flicked the light switch on and a low soft yellow light bulb came on. The cellar was large and dark, with boxes and crates stacked into every crevice. They sighed, realising that it could take hours to sort through it all.

As they were moving boxes, Jay remembered the first day, when he thought he saw himself in a mirror, but nothing was there. He went back to the doorway and looked in at the same angle. He was looking at some boxes of crisps stacked up against a stone wall.

Den was watching him,

"What?" he asked.

Jay told him what he was thinking and they both started to move the crisp boxes to one side and as soon as they did, the light reflected straight back from an old heavy mirror leaning against the wall. Den slapped Jay on the back, and together they lifted the mirror out of the corner.

As they raised it, thick dense cobwebs pulled away behind, and surprised black spiders scurried away into dark corners. The ancient mirror had dark spots all over it and hardly gave a reflection at all.

"Let's put it back over the fireplace" grunted Den, trying to lift it,

"Why?"

"Cos that's where his wife would have looked in the mirror, there must be something in the reflection."

Den did not reply but seemed open to this idea.

John watched the boys as they went past him, struggling with the huge mirror trailing webs in their wake. Den smiled at him as they went past; trying to look as though they were behaving normally.

They dragged a tall barstool over to the fireplace and balanced the mirror on top of it, in front of the fireplace and then they both stood there and looked at themselves in the mirror.

John raised an eyebrow.

Behind them, all they could see was the back wall, tables and chairs. Nothing. No clues. They sat down.

"If you've quite finished," said John, "you could both load them bottles of lager in the fridge."

The boys had to agree in the end that there was nothing to see in the mirror now, and that although their first guess was probably correct, that they needed to look in the reflection of the mirror in 1790 rather than now. The boys sat in silence; this meant another trip back into the dream.

Getting no response from the two boys, John threw down the dishcloth muttering,

"I give up." and he went out to get the lagers himself.

– Chapter 20 –

DANIEL

The boys returned to Jay's cottage in silence – going back into the dream felt a lot less exciting than the last time. They sat in his room with the buckle on the floor in the middle of the room.

"We could ask Mother Blight to stay in the room and watch over us, to make sure we come back." said Den, but actually remembering that she didn't ever want to see them again.

Jay shook his head,

"We go alone, but make sure that Katie is locked out of the room this time."

Den nodded. "But we don't have another crystal to come back with." he said,

"I wasn't going to use one the first time," Jay replied, pushing the buckle thoughtfully with his foot, "you were supposed to take the herbs out from under the pillow to wake me up."

"I know, but you need me with you to keep you out of trouble."

"No I don't."

"Yes you do."

"No I don't."

Then a third voice:

"Yes he does!" – They turned and saw Jay's twelve year old younger brother Daniel standing in the doorway.

"Or even both of us to keep you out of trouble." Daniel grinned.

Jay was shaking his head, Den was laughing. Daniel had Jay's dark brown eyes and hair, but was slighter in build, quieter, less impulsive than Jay.

"What do you think you know?" Jay asked,

"Well," replied Daniel sitting down on the carpet and picking up the buckle, "I know everything that Katie just told me and everything I just heard you both saying."

"Butt out Danny," Jay said "it's not real."

Daniel continued to study the buckle.

"Well," he replied thoughtfully, "Logically none of this makes any sense, but then again, it didn't sound like you were joking."

Katie who had been listening at the door ran in shouting,

"It's true, it's true, cross my heart and everything, I'm not lying!"

Jay sighed and pulled his little sister onto his lap,

"OK." he said, "OK, be quiet now" – and Daniel winked at Katie, and sat back and waited for the full story.

Chapter 21

BACK TO MOTHER BLIGHT

It was five o'clock, and the three boys had left Katie with the next door neighbour who was a family friend, and wandered down to the pier to buy chips. Already the tired sun was retreating, and the grey skies of a winter's evening were creeping over the town.

The boys shivered, they were sitting on the edge of an old stonewall in the small fishing port, feet dangling free over the long drop into the choppy sea below. The tourists were packing up; no longer amused by catching small crabs, pretending to scream and then throwing them back in.

"This whole 'time-dreaming' thing," said Den, tossing small stones into the sea, "What do we really know about it?"

"Not much," replied Jay eventually, "we were just playing around."

"So?" asked Den

"So …" Jay stood up, "So we had better go and find out more before one of us gets killed." Daniel didn't like the sound of that, but followed them anyway.

It was not far to Mother Blight's sea front cottage, but they walked slowly, not really wanting to arrive. Den raised his hand to lift the doorknocker, but the door swung open before he could. Mother Blight was not pleased to see them. She nodded as a greeting and opened the door for them to enter the small cottage, frowning at Daniel when she saw that they had now been joined by another boy.

It was modern, clean and tidy, full of books and bottles made of coloured glass that reflected around the room. There were a lot of cats lazing around, that appeared to be sleeping, but were actually watching the visitors very closely.

"You want a drink?" she asked rather abruptly. Jay shook his head,

Mother Blight sat on the sofa and waited for the other boys to sit, Den was looking at some photos of her daughter Bonnie on the side table.

"So?" she said, snatching the photo away, "What do you want?"

"We want to know everything," Jay said. "About the dreams."

Mother Blight frowned. She looked out of the small lead light windows,

"I told you it was not something to take lightly." she said seriously.

"Yes. Sorry." muttered Jay.

They waited, and eventually Mother Blight began to talk in a quiet voice.

"It's a Pengelli thing," she said, "Always was these powers in them. It has been known for hundreds of years."

Daniel leaned over as if to say something, but she scowled so terrifyingly at him that he just sat back in his chair. She continued:

"Others can join in, as you have discovered, but only a Pengelli can have the power. As I said before, you need to be a direct blood link to someone in the dream and to hold an item linked directly to their time, untarnished by any other hands."

She paused, and sighed, before continuing,

"Some Pengelli's can master the power so well, that they no longer need the item with them to go back, and that they can eventually come and go at will. Of course, there is great danger, some get lost in the adventure of it and forget to come back. Some die there and no-one knows. This is not a gift – this is a curse – you should rue the day you found that belt buckle."

Jay waited until it seemed that she had finished and said,

"How? How can I master it? How can I go back into the dreams and return on my own?"

"You don't want to know – it will cost you a bit of your soul each time that you do."

By now Daniel had had enough, he stood up and touched Jays arm,

"Let's go." he said "This stuff's too weird." but Jay did not respond to him and shook off his hand.

"Please." Jay said to Mother Blight ignoring Daniel, "I need to know, I need to help my family."

Mother Blight stood up. Thinking. Looking at them. The watery winter sun was setting outside, and through the window, thin shards of pale yellow light reflected in her eyes – it seemed as though her piercing green eyes were on fire.

"Not now." she said. Jay did not move. She sighed.

"Fine." she snapped, "If you really want to know about the Pengelli's powers, it's simply this - every time you go back, your powers will increase. At first you won't be able to control them – you will be jumping in and out of dreams without even wanting to. You will pass by something familiar then BAM you're in the dreams, then before you know it BAM you're back again!"

The boys were jumping every time she shouted BAM and slammed her hand on the table.

"Why do you want such a thing? Young boys like you? Next thing you know and BAM you're all dead!"

Silence. They just looked at each other.

"That's useful to know." said Daniel. Den chuckled until Mother Blight glared at him.

"But how can I practise then?" Jay persisted. Mother Blight stood up,

"I've no idea; I'm not a Pengelli, so how should I know? My advice is to give the buckle to me to get rid of it for you and then you young boys forget all this craziness. If you want to earn money for your family, then go and get a paper round."

She leaned forward to take the buckle but Jay lifted it away.

"Thank you." he said politely.

Something was troubling Jay though, something in the back of his mind, and even after they had left the cottage and walked home, it remained there niggling away – something she had said? Something he had seen? Something familiar? Couldn't quite work it out

Chapter 22

THREE GO INTO THE DREAM

They were back - this time the dream had taken three boys.

They were prepared for the storm and ducked down from the stinging rain. Then as one - they ran full out towards the cave. They felt as though they were running through a war zone, but only Daniel was surprised and shocked by the brutality of the dream.

As they approached the cave, they saw Mad Matt on the floor and Jack leaving, just as before.

Daniel tripped over someone on the sand and seeing that they were being robbed – he stopped to shout at the thief. The thief was pure evil, a short ugly man, the few hairs left on his head were being blown around in the storm like crazy dancing grass, but even when the moonlight cut through for a moment, there was still no light in his eyes.

The thief paused, knife in one hand, the victim's pocket watch in the other. Daniel and the man faced each other for just a moment, and then the thief was gone. Looking down at the wounded man, Daniel could see that he had gone as well – but from this world. Daniel glared after the vanished thief – he would not forget that face.

They had only one aim – to reach the Inn, look at the reflection in the mirror, see where the treasure was hidden, then get straight back home again.

Jay had a crystal in his pocket – and yes they had gone back to Mother Blight, and yes she was very angry and yes she did in the end give Den a handful of the crystals and yes she told them never to come back to her door again!

It didn't seem to matter to anyone in the dream that the boys were in modern day clothes, maybe because it was just a dream. With Den leading, the boys made their way along the long and dark passageway to the Inn.

They expected the Inn to be full, but it was empty, every man was out on the beach watching or looting or rescuing – depending upon the goodness of their soul, and luckily for the souls on the stricken ship, there were more angels than devils on the beach that night.

It was only once their eyes became accustomed to the flickering candles, that the boys saw the Innkeeper standing behind the bar. He glared over at Den, he could see a family resemblance, but the boys just ignored him and walked across to the mirror above the blazing fire.

Two soaking wet men suddenly burst into the pub with several small barrels of rum. The Innkeeper called over to them,

"Bring them out back to the Kiddleywink!" he commanded and they disappeared out to the back of the Inn.

"Kiddley what now?" said Daniel. The others shrugged.

Basically, looking in the mirror did nothing to help, it was too dark. Jay took a candle from a table and held it up. The three boys saw themselves in the reflection of the old mirror, flickering in the candlelight.

Over their shoulders they could all see one thing – on the back wall behind them was a little painting of a stack of large rocks on the moors. They looked closer, and underneath was neatly written 'Cheesering'.

Just then, two of the Squire's men burst in. They called out to the Inn keeper, shouting that they were looking for the Squire's daughter dressed in a black coat and blue silk dress, but the men in the Inn just shrugged and continued with their work of hiding the barrels of rum.

The men saw the boys and ran towards them, daggers drawn, but as they approached, there was the sound of crystal smashing on the ground and the boys vanished and returned home.

– Chapter 23 –

THE CHEESERING

In the local tourist office, it only took the boys a few minutes to find twenty or more books and pictures about the stack of ancient stones in Bodmin Moor called the Cheesewring. Huge ancient Stone Age monuments, standing silently on the moors, oblong rocks shaped like smooth grey biscuits, all stacked precariously on top of one other.

And later that day as the boys clambered over the hills, they immediately recognised the Cheesewring from quite a distance. Den had known these stones all his life, had played on them with his friends on long summer afternoons, but didn't know they had a name.

A couple of tourists were circling the monument and taking photographs. The boys sat on a nearby hill until they rambled on, and then they approached the stones and walked around them.

For an hour they climbed, examined, dug and generally searched for anything that might be a hint to the treasure, but they found nothing.

"Whatever it was will probably be long gone after two hundred years." Jay sighed,

"Long shot anyway." Den said.

The boys lay on the stones as the sun started to set.

"We need to get home, it's dangerous here at night." Daniel warned. But Jay was looking at the buckle; he was turning it over and over in his hands.

"I hope you're not thinking, what I think you're thinking?" Daniel said to him.

"What?" asked Den. Daniel shook his head,

"He's thinking of going back into the dream now, to see if he can arrive when Jack is hiding the stuff in the stones."

They were all silent. They all had the same thoughts – dangerous – stupid – might work!

Jay decided to go back into the dream alone – Den and Daniel stayed back to guard him. He closed his eyes and imagined the moors at night, this very spot with Jack and then….

Suddenly Jay was very cold. It was so dark that he could not even see his hands in front of him. Instinctively he crouched down low and stayed still until his eyes became somewhat accustomed to the absolute darkness.

He shivered violently, the air was frosty and the grass underneath him was soft and wet. He tried to make sense of his surroundings, but he was disorientated and confused.

The air smelt of damp earth. There were scuffling sounds from small animals nearby, and the eerie whistling of the wind across the moors, ran through him like an icy ghost.

If he looked up, the black sky was full of millions of bright stars, far brighter than in modern times, and he wondered at the beauty of it until something else caught his eye.

There was a tiny flickering light in the distance, sometimes visible, sometimes not, but gradually getting bigger and nearer. Jay moved back away from the Cheesewring and hid behind a cluster of bushes nearby.

As the flickering light came closer it was clearly a candle or lantern of some kind, until finally the darkness parted and the outline of a giant man came into view, a frightening and familiar figure.

Jay was scared even to look at this man after the last time they had met, when Jack had pointed a loaded pistol at him and pulled the trigger.

Jack approached the stones. He looked back to see if anyone had followed him, and then sat down to rest. He was breathing so heavily that Jay could hear him from behind the bushes, and held his own breath in case he could also be heard.

After a while, he could hear digging – Jack had brought a small shovel, and was digging under the stones. He seemed to dig for ages, until Jay could just about see that he had dug a hole at least three feet deep, before dropping a small wooden box into the hole and then re-filling and stamping the soil back into place.

As Jack stamped on the earth he appeared to become more and more angry, and then he looked up at the sky and roared,

"Damn 'yee Matt Crowle, yeel'll not get my fortune and yee''ll not betray me agin!"

Jay watched in horror as Jack pulled out his knife and sliced it through the palm of his own hand. Blood dripped down onto the stones, and then Jack shouted once more,

"I swear on my blood, I will have 'ee return my gold or I'll cut out yer black heart!"

Jay daren't even breathe; he had never witnessed such fury. As he watched Jack stamping the ground and cursing to the moors, he now understood the sudden break up of Matt and Jack, and how Matt came to be murdered in the cave that night by his own partner and lifelong friend.

Jay awoke while Jack was walking away, and he had the sense that Jack was broken by this betrayal.

– Chapter 24 –

KEEP DIGGING

It was now so dark on the moors that the boys had to wait until the next day to return to look for the buried box.

In daylight, Jay smiled to see that he could easily identify the exact spot where Jack had buried the box. They had brought shovels with them, but as the Cheesewring was a protected monument, they kept watch for ramblers and tourists in case they were seen.

The ground was hard, and as they took in turns to dig, Jay was impressed at the strength and stamina of Jack, who had dug this up by himself.

They dug down to three feet, but found nothing. Deciding that maybe the box had sunk lower over time, they kept going – but there was nothing there.

After two hours, the boys sat down in silence feeling defeated and disappointed.

"OK, let's fill it in." said Den, wiping a muddy hand across his sweaty face.

"I'll do it." said Jay. He picked up the shovel, but as he lifted the first pile of earth to thrown into the hole he blacked out....

For a moment he was back in darkness, he was back in the dream, Jack was cursing, but this time Jay was looking down into the hole – and far down he could see the small box at the very bottom of the muddy hole.

Jay shot back to the present, he was lying on the grass and the boys were trying to wake him up.

"Jay, Jay wake up!" Daniel was shouting while shaking his shoulders.

Jay was on the ground, he was disoriented and confused. How did that happen? Now he was just flying in and out of dreams without any control or warning.

Jay sat up, a bit dazed, and then eventually he smiled.

"It's in there," he said, "We haven't dug deep enough yet."

And sure enough, another eighteen inches down and the shovel hit something, and the boys pulled out what was left of a small leather bag.

Even though the box had almost entirely disintegrated, the leather pouch inside was just about holding together, preserved by the peat in the ground.

They waited a moment, not wanting to look inside in case this was a big disappointment. But then, Jay pulled the ties apart and tipped out the contents onto the flat rock surface.

It was full of small stones, some cut and some rough, but it was obvious that these were rubies. The sun caught the red reflective light immediately and shone it brilliantly into their eyes. They were dazzling and worth a small fortune.

– Chapter 25 –

SMUGGLING

(In the past 1790 - a month before the storm.)

Four weeks before the storm, Wrecker Jack and Mad Matt were leaning against a rough stone wall near a small cove known as Rum Bay.

These two men were large dark figures, feared and respected by the locals, and even the Squire was careful around them. They had reputations as ruthless smugglers, without a soul or honour some say, and certainly murderers and thieves of the worst kind. They had but one friend in the world and that was each other – but all that was about to end with the temptation of a King's ransom in solid gold.

They were waiting for one of the Squire's smuggling vessels to arrive, and had put out the word that tub men were needed to carry goods from the ship, and were expecting more than a hundred men and women from nearby to help to unload the boat.

It was early morning, very quiet and the fog lay low upon the land and water. Every breath produced swirls of white mist, which floated around carrying the men's whispers out to sea.

Rum Bay harbour was so sheltered and secluded that it was impossible to see what boats were there unless someone literally leaned over the edge of the cliff above. It was cut out of solid rock with one roadway climbing up the face of the cliff on one side of the cave. The rocks were full of small caves, some with their openings built up to connect to the houses above by secret passages.

On that misty morning, a hundred and thirty men and women were waiting patiently with donkeys and ponies for the cutter to arrive. Many of the men were sitting on the rocks smoking small clay pipes, while the women took advantage of the free time to knit large woollen jumpers – each knitted with their own unique family pattern - so that the bodies of the fishermen could be identified if they drowned out at sea.

The Cornish fishermen at that time were extremely poor because of the Kings taxes. Most were God-fearing and law abiding, but if the Excise men came by to try to stop them unloading from the ships, then the fishermen were armed with sticks and hangers (swords) if they needed to fight for their lives.

The coastguard had been decoyed by the Squire to a distant part of their district by rumours of smuggling there. When they were sure that the coast was clear, the smugglers ship cast anchor near the shore. The entire town turned out when Jack and Matt were bringing in smuggled booty from across the sea.

Unusually, the Squire was also there to oversee the unloading of the cargo of tea, tobacco, rum, lace, silk, and brandy. He was there in particular that day to protect the thirty ton cutter's additional cargo of a hundred cakes of copper, ten blocks of silver bullion and two hundred gold coins.

The Squire had brought with him his own small army of twenty men, armed with hangers and pistols, to ensure that the copper, gold and silver were taken directly to his Manor.

Small rowing boats ferried to and fro from the cutter bringing in the goods, which were then slung onto the backs of donkeys and moved along in long lines, or carried on the strong shoulders of the men and women.

The kegs were then carried away and stored in hiding holes and under gardens, in cellars or up in attics. Many of the fishermen's houses had secret shafts, chambers in walls, concealment under floors and behind cupboards with false backs.

Before the short day in January was done, the little ship was nearly cleared and the goods hidden away.

"Sarchers!" Matt suddenly growled, and all eyes turned to the fast approaching boat in the distance. Out of the misty gloom swept the long boat of the coastguard close upon them. Eight armed men shouting at them to surrender in the Kings name.

One of the excise men fired his pistol and the bullet whistled near to one of the men on board the Squires ship. The water flew from the eight oars that now gave chase. Thrusting out a boat hook, one excise man tried to seize the cutter but failed when the Squires men cut the line with his sword.

Everyone on the shore immediately dispersed as though they had never been there, they ran silently and the sight was mystical as the crowded beach emptied in moments.

The Sarchers (searchers/excise men) had found them, or been tipped off. These were the loyal men who were not in the pocket of the Squire. Matt and Jack stood ready to fight, and in fact always looked forward to it. Jack smiled as he drew his pistol in one hand and a dagger in the other.

They knew though that it was unlikely that there would be a fight today – there were only eight of the Kings men, and they would not be foolish enough to take on twenty of the Squires men, why the two of them could take only eight men by themselves! No the Kings men would just pretend to chase the smugglers and then run back home.

– Chapter 26 –

GOLD

The squire mounted his horse, and took off urgently with his men behind him. The smugglers on board the cutter saw that everyone else had run away, and so set sail to the open sea, firing at the excise men and laughing as they made their getaway.

The excise men could see they were outmanned and outgunned, and did not make too much effort to follow the cutter out to sea. Jack fired his pistol into the air, and he laughed with Matt as the Kings men turned their boat around and raced back to the other shore.

As the Squires men raced away from the customs men, they did not notice that four bags had fallen down from the backs of the horses in their haste to get away. Matt and Jack saw it though, and having no fear of the Squire or the King's men, they waded out into the incoming tide and collected them up.

Matt and Jack stood in the rain with the wind whipping around them and stared at the gold in the bags. This was a real fortune, this was enough gold for them to retire – even be Squires themselves if they had a mind to it.

Both greedy men thought that it would be even better if they didn't have to share, and it was at that moment that the seeds to the end of their friendship began to grow like a poisonous weed.

In case anyone else was about, they hurried off into the dark cave and then tipped the coins onto the floor. They were heavy; the large gold coins sank into the damp sand, reflecting back like sharp sunlight.

Four bags of gold, two hundred coins in total - so heavy that the strong smugglers could not have carried them far without using a pony or horse. They knew they had to act quickly; the Squire would soon be back with his men, tearing the beach apart to find the gold.

"Too much fortune for one man." Matt was muttering, Jack nodded – but neither really thought so.

After a few moments of being mesmerised by the gold, they came to their senses, and started to drag the bags to the back of the cave where they had hidden treasure before. Pulling out large loose black wet stones, they opened a space in the rocks and shoved the bags into the hole and then filled it up again with the rocks. Both men were sweating with the effort,

"Gotta leave it there," Jack was saying "Squire'll find out if we spend it too quick."

Matt laughed, showing his missing teeth, he mimed having his throat cut and laughed even more. Jack watched his friend and smiled, knowing that he wouldn't hesitate for a second to take it all when the time came.

The seawater started to seep into the cave, and the men knew the dangers of getting trapped with the tides – they turned as one, and walked away from the gold hidden there in the dark.

Two sets of eyes were on them while this had happened. The first was from someone who had also seen the gold fall into the sea, and then followed them into the cave. This person was silently laughing in the shadows.

Secondly far away in time, Jay was in a deep sleep and his dreams had found their way to this moment, and he hovered like a spirit at the top of the cave, looking down at where the gold was hidden. And yet, Jay could not see who the shadowy figure hiding in the cave was.

– Chapter 27 –

GOLD HUNTING

Based on the dream, the boys knew that the treasure had been hidden at the far end of the cave in Rum Bay. Den and Jay decided to go down after dark when tourists would not be around, just in case the gold was still there, even though it was not very likely.

The sea was not being kind tonight. The waves roared and rolled at speed, crashing into rocks and lashing at the shore, at war with the earth. Even the seagulls were silent, which made the immense sound of the sea even more intense, and the waves and black sky and the screaming gale force wind, filled every part of the shore and sea.

Wet and numbed Den and Jay crept about in the dark cave on the wet sandy floor, aware that the sea was already washing around their ankles. They felt nervous being out in this storm, and hurried to the back of the cave to see quickly if the gold was still there.

It took just a few moments to see that there was a gaping hole at the back, the loose rocks removed many years ago, and certainly nothing was hidden in this cave now.

Suddenly the light in the cave was darkened, and there was a deafening boom and a dreadful rushing in of salty air. The cave was high roofed and deep with a narrow and low entrance. The tide had risen; each wave swept over the mouth driving in the air that flew back again with the boom of a cannon firing, when the wave began to recede. Soon the cave itself would be filled with icy seawater.

They realised their error and jeopardy immediately. They had to get out before the tide came in fully or they would drown. The water was now lapping around their legs, and suddenly the peril was critical, the speed of the incoming tide was terrifying.

They waded back out towards the entrance and could already see that the freezing cold waves were pouring onto the shore with force.

The sand beneath their feet started to shift, they no longer felt as though they were on solid ground, but trying to swim or be swept off their feet now, would be most certainly be fatal, as the outwash of the tide would drag them out to sea.

Nature had cut them off by a huge granite hill, surrounded by dangerous tidal creeks and so rough and dangerous that nobody went there went the tide was in. At least in a dream he could have woken up, but they had come here in present time and the danger was real.

Den was scrambling onto the outlining rocks above the entrance of the cave, Jay followed, but the rocks were slippery with water and seaweed, and now the salt air was in their eyes. It would only take one strong wave to wrench them from the rocks and then it would all be over.

Den was incredibly strong, and climbed like an ape, slow but effortlessly, upwards and sideways along the jutting rocks; Jay was struggling but determined to keep up.

By keeping close to Den, Jay was protected from the brunt of the powerful wind blowing in from the sea, and even though he couldn't see where he was going, he trusted Den and stayed close.

The sea boomed again into the cave and the shock caused Jay to slip, his feet sliding downwards. In panic he gripped the slippery stones and desperately tried to get a grip with his toes on the wet stones, but just as he felt he was going to fall, Den's strong hand gripped his wrist and somehow hauled him back onto safe footing.

Then they heard shouting, and looking up saw two fishermen calling down to them to hold on. The brave men climbed down to meet them and with their help, the boys crawled back onto solid land and lay there shivering.

"You alright now then?" one man asked,

They nodded, and then the two fishermen walked away before the boys even had a chance to get their breath back or thank them.

– Chapter 28 –

SQUIRE AT THE INN

(In the past – before the storm)

The Squire sat in the corner of the tavern in the dark shadows. From here he could observe everyone in the low-beamed room, and also hear everything they had to say – even the whispers. The firelight gave off an ominous flickering orange light, and when he leaned forward, his evil face lit up like a devil in hell.

He tightly gripped his own silver tankard, which he always brought with him, and every half an hour, a barmaid would fill it from a jug of ale without being asked and without being thanked.

An argument broke out somewhere nearby, loud rough voices. The Squire smiled, he knew them, it was Jack and Matt, they came in every night and always ended up drunk and fighting. But then the tone changed, it sounded more serious, more personal, the Squire sat up and listened more carefully, his instincts were telling him that this was interesting.

Something was being said about gold and greed, but just as the subject was really getting interesting, two young sailors walked over to the fire to warm their hands, standing in front of the fireplace between the Squire and the two arguing smugglers.

The Squire slammed his tankard down on the table and shouted,

"Get away dogs!" The two sailors both turned, ready for a fight, but from another other dark corner three large, armed men stepped into the firelight and just stood there, they made it very clear with their body language that it would be a mistake to take on this fight.

The sailors pretended that they didn't care, one spat into the fire, but then they both turned and walked away, and the three bodyguards melted away back silently into the blackness.

The argument between Matt and Jack became more violent – they were shoving each other and cursing. Both of them drew their daggers but the men from the tavern pulled them apart and ordered them to leave.

Luckily for the barmen, Matt and Jack thought it best to take their private business outside; otherwise there would have been bloodshed that night.

Chapter 29

WHERE'S THE GOLD?

Jay was trying to decide whether to attempt another dream. He didn't want to keep involving his family, because every time that he did, it was always dangerous. But then again, he and Den still managed to almost get themselves killed by looking for the gold when awake!

He turned the buckle over in his hands as he sat on the edge of his bed; he just wanted to know about the gold, what exactly happened between Jack and Matt? A lifetime of friendship, then it was all over so suddenly and violently, and he wondered if the gold was still around and hidden somewhere nearby. As long as Jack had known where it was hidden, then he should be able to find out.

Jay thought that if he concentrated on Jack and Matt fighting, then maybe he would arrive at a time when the secrets would be revealed.

With a crystal in his pocket, Jay lay down and imagined Jack and Matt arguing about gold, he imagined shouting and anger and the two smugglers attacking each other, gold coins and the crashing sea and then - he was back…

It was night time in the small fishing town and pitch black. Tiny flickering lights sat in some of the small windows, the waves lashed onto the shore and the clip clop of ponies on nearby cobbled streets echoed in the air. No rain, but a freezing wind was blowing in from the sea, and despite a brilliant white moon, the town was dark and ominous.

Jay was in a side street, he couldn't really get his bearings because it was so dark, until he heard the loud voice of Jack behind him, and turning around he recognised the Inn. It must have been late evening, the Inn was full and small candles flickered on the tables, and there was the clinking of glasses and the general clamour of talking and laughing.

Jack was in the street with Matt and they were drunk and arguing. The Inn Keeper was at the door and had just kicked them out with the help of several men,

"Wee'll sort it _now!_" Jack was shouting, he was slurring his words, they were both really drunk.

"Now and fer good!" Matt growled back.

The smugglers both looked at the skies as though checking how the night was going to be, and then they started to stagger away from the town and towards the caves on the shore.

Jay followed; it was easy at night, so dark that he could hardly even see his own feet, and the crashing waves wiped out any sounds of footsteps.

On they went, occasionally steering drunkenly to the side of the road, then laughing or cursing before carrying on. Down to the beach and into the cave they went, not once looking back to see if they were being followed – firstly because they were too drunk and secondly because they did not believe that anyone would dare.

As Jack and Matt staggered into the cave, Jay ran in after them and hid behind a huge overhanging rock. The tide was out, and

Matt lit a small candle or lantern that threw a dim light into the deep darkness of the cave.

Jay started to shiver violently in the freezing cold, and he envied the huge dark coats that the smugglers wore. Matt was at the far end of the cave pulling away rocks, but after a moment or two there was a shout that sounded like a roar when the two men found that the gold was missing.

The fury of the two men was truly terrifying. Jay stepped back as they swore and screamed at each other and started to fight. It felt like giants raging in the echoing chambers of the rocks, and Jay decided to get out of there fast – if they should see him now, he would stand no chance.

Jay smashed the crystal on the rocks and closed his eyes – but nothing happened. Why? That should work, why didn't it work? Did the witch do this to him on purpose?

Nothing happened except that the fighting brutes heard the high pitched sound of glass breaking and turned immediately to him.

In absolute terror Jay closed his eyes and thought of home, he did not open his eyes even when he heard them running up to him, he frantically thought 'Home! Home! Home!'

And just in time he awoke in his room, his hair matted with sweat and he was shaking with terror.

Jay sat on his bed – so the gold was stolen from the thieves, ironic. That's why the men fought, that's why Jack killed Matt in the end, because he just couldn't believe that anyone else would dare to steal from him.

Chapter 30

KATIE'S DOG

A few days had passed since the discovery of the rubies, but the boys did not know what to do with them. Crazy Uncle Joss had still not been detained by the police, but had been seen ranting and raving about town looking for the boys and his 'treasure'.

Den had discovered a new girlfriend and they hadn't seen him for two days, and so Daniel and Jay had to decide whether to tell their Mum everything – did they even own the rubies? Even if they belonged to Jack, had he stolen them in the first place? And even if they decided to go to the police, can you imagine their reaction to the story!

Their Mum Trisha returned, tired, upset, in no mood to talk to anyone. She had arrived back with their sister Natasha, and then immediately taken off again to visit someone else; apparently she had been trying to borrow money from all the family members that she could track down.

Daniel and Jay made a decision, they were going to have one more talk with the witch to ask her advice, as she seemed to know everything, but they felt that she was still holding something back. Rather than take Katie with them, they took the reckless decision to leave her on her own in the cottage for half an hour, she seemed to be ok with that, what could possibly go wrong?

Katie liked to play with the pretty red stones. She knew they were valuable and secret, and so when the boys went out, they told her to hide the small bag of rubies in her nightdress case. It was a white fluffy dog with a zip on the back, and she crammed the treasure in there and put it back under her pillow.

Katie sat alone on her bed. She had knots in her stomach and wanted to be sick.

She wanted to be brave but she was keenly aware of her age and size compared to Den's Uncle Joss. She nervously chewed the ends of her long wavy brown hair and closed her eyes. She remembered being lost on the beach and the kind lady rescuing her. She remembered Jay finding her and bringing her safely home, she remembered Den being there as well, and she felt stronger.

Someone was outside in the yard. Katie froze with terror and clutched the dog to her, jumping as small pebbles hit the window. Katie tiptoed over and peeked through the curtains and peered down to see who it was.

"Oh," she whispered "it's you," and she smiled.

Just a brief moment later, Katie and the rubies were gone.

– Chapter 31 –

TEXT MESSAGES

The boys had already decided that leaving Katie was too risky and had turned around and returned to the house.

Katie was gone. They had only been away ten minutes. There was a message left on the table, it simply read:

'Katie for rubies. Wait for text.'

– whoever wrote it didn't realise that they already had the jewels inside Katie's toy, but that was even more dangerous because if they found this out, then there may not be any need to keep Katie safe?

Jay knew straight away – the only person who knew that there were rubies in the house was Den. He was the only other person who Katie would have trusted.

Daniel tried to calm him down, but Jay was fit to explode with rage, he pushed passed his brother as though he were made of paper, and stormed out of the house towards the Inn. Daniel decided to stay in case she returned there, but made some phone calls as he watched his brother running down to the Inn.

Jay struggled to run down the cobbled streets, the wind gusted and tugged at his hair and clothes, and cut at his face like cold sharp knives. He could not believe the betrayal. He could not cope with the lies. He could not breathe with this traitor in his life, in his world.

Now he understood real fury, the need to destroy bad stuff in his life, and he understood how righting wrongs may mean being wrong yourself, crossing the line and not knowing if you can ever come back. He was glad of the rain, the icy rain hid his crying eyes – cold tears of fury and frustration and hatred.

Jay burst into the Inn, drenched with rain and with fire in his eyes; he stood a moment, looking around in fury. John was behind the bar; he looked at him in alarm,

"What the hell..." he started to say, when Jay demanded,

"Where's Den?"

"He went out about an hour ago, I thought he was with you lad." John said,

"Yeah," said Jay, "I thought he was with me too." Just then Jay heard a text beep on his phone, the message read:

'Bench on pier by boat trips, 10 mins, bring stuff and leave on bench.'

Jay stared at the message; he wanted to smash it against the wall. He texted back:

'Ok. Hurt her and you're dead'

There was a couple of seconds delay, and then the return text was a smiley. Jay shook with rage, the traitor was smiling at him and the answerback on the phone was Den.

John came out from behind the bar, but before he could ask any questions, Jay slammed open the door and stormed back out into the rain.

It was then that he faintly heard the phone ringing in his pocket. He ignored it, didn't want to play. But then, instinct warned him that he should answer it, so he pulled out his phone, and listened and then stopped dead in the middle of the street, frozen to the spot.

– Chapter 32 –

FIGHT WITH A TRAITOR

The call was from Den's crazy Uncle Joss. He was shouting down the phone something about being near his cottage and that he was coming to get him or any of this family to beat the location of the treasure out of them. He didn't let Jay speak, he was just shouting and ranting and Jay would have hung up if the threat to his brother hadn't been so real.

Joss was going to his house and Daniel was there. Joss hung up. Jay dialled and re-dialled the house and Daniel's mobile, but Daniel's mobile number was engaged, and no-one was answering the house phone. While the panic and fury in him was fit to explode. He sent warning texts to Daniel then had to stop trying.

Jay was torn. Daniel was alone facing a crazy man, and Katie was missing again. He knew that there was no choice, he could not even begin to think about saving Daniel - he at least had a fighting chance, however slim, but Katie had no chance at all by herself. His sigh was as deep as the ocean; Jay turned away from his brother, and began to run at speed to rescue his sister.

Then he saw him – Den was sitting on a low wall eating an ice-cream. Jay actually wanted to kill him, that smug, betraying, lying, piece of scum.

As Jay ran up to him, Den smiled. That was the final straw, Jay threw himself at him, and although Den was far bigger than Jay, he was taken by surprise and thrown to the ground. They scuffled in the muddy street, Jay trying to punch Den, and Den just holding him off. He was too strong for Jay, but was only just able to hold him back because of the blind fury.

Jay was shouting,

"Where is she? Tell me now, where is she!" Then Jay felt himself being pulled backwards by the very strong arms of John Crowle who had followed Jay, and now hauled him off his son and pinned his arms back behind him.

"What the hell?" John demanded. Den was shaking; he was just staring at Jay in shock.

"Him!" Jay was ranting "he's a liar, he's a kidnapper, he's a .."

"What you talking about?" Den was trying to say in between Jays ranting. John was not going to let Jay go while he was still struggling, so eventually Jay stopped and glared at Den.

"Tell him!" Jay demanded, "Tell your Dad what you've done! Where is she?"

"You've gone mad mate," Den said, wiping dirt of his shirt, "Where's who gone?"

"Katie!" Jay shouted, trying again to pull free from John to attack Den again.

"Stop it or you'll get hurt lad." John warned him.

"I need to get to my phone" Jay said. John let him go, but stood between the two of them just in case. Jay pulled out the mobile with the last text messages on and gave it to John. He frowned and past it to Den asking

"What's this lad?"

Den stared at the messages, he looked shocked. He looked at Jay and understood.

"I didn't send this Jay." he said, "I don't have my mobile any more".

Everything spun around in Jay's head. It was a simple enough statement, but he could tell it was the truth. What the hell was going on?

Jay slowly slumped down onto the low wall. Katie was taken by someone else. Joss was on his way to Daniel. Nothing made sense, no-one knew about the rubies except him and Den. Then he noticed Den's expression – he had clearly remembered something and had that same look that Jay had had earlier.

"What?" Jay said, Den shook his head and replied,

"Sorry man, it's my fault, she took my phone, and I told her everything"

"Who? Told who?"

"I thought she liked me.

"Who?!" Jay was on his feet and shaking Den by the shirt; Den looked at his friend and said,

"My girlfriend. Bonnie Blight. The witch's daughter."

As Den said that name Jay suddenly saw it all – in the dream, the little cottage where Katie had been, it was the same witches cottage. It wasn't the Squire's daughter in the blue dress, it was the witch's daughter, it was someone that Katie would trust and was too small to understand that it wasn't the same person just because they looked the same.

The photo in the witch's house, Bonnie looked exactly like the witches daughter in the dream. Katie would have trusted Bonnie Blight

Chapter 33

FINDING KATIE AGAIN

Bonnie and Katie sat in a coffee shop overlooking the sea. Katie was happily eating chips with ketchup, and telling her friend Bonnie long childish stories that Bonnie was not listening to.

Katie was sitting with her back to the window, and so only Bonnie could see Den and Jay through the window silently fighting on the pier behind her. Bonnie smiled, Katie thought that she was smiling at her stories and so told her some more.

It was whilst Bonnie was watching the boys fighting, and then watching Den's Dad drag them apart, that she thought she heard Katie say something about 'pretty stones'.

"Katie dear," Bonnie said, "Tell me again about the pretty stones?"

Katie bit her bottom lip, she wasn't supposed to tell, but then, she wasn't supposed to tell bad people, but this was her friend.

Shyly Katie brought out her toy dog from under the table and unzipped the back, inside Bonnie could see a small bag.

"Show me." Bonnie whispered. Katie looked around, and then pulled open the little bag so that the shiny red rubies could be seen by her friend. Bonnie laughed and thought to herself 'Excellent'.

"I think," said Bonnie, "that I should look after those for you, and that way you don't have to worry about losing them?"

Katie shook her head at first, but then in her young mind, she had been scared to look after them, and Bonnie was a grown up. After a little while she handed over the small bag, and happily returned to eating her chips.

Bonnie took out Den's phone and prepared a short text message. Then she stood up and said,

"Katie, I am just going to the toilet, will you be ok for a few minutes?" Katie nodded, still fully engrossed in dipping chips into ketchup.

Bonnie ducked out the back entrance, and once in her car and driving out of the town she took out the mobile and pressed 'send' to Jay:

'Cheers Jay, you can collect your prize from the Pier Café'

And Bonnie laughed out loud as she put her foot down speeding towards the motorway.

Jay read the message and spun around towards the café, where he could see Katie in the window of the Café on the pier. He pointed her out to Den and showed him the text, telling him to get Katie. Den and John promised that they would take care of Katie and then Jay had to go. He couldn't wait any longer; he had to run home to see if Daniel was OK.

Jay had reached the top of the hill when he glanced back to the town and saw Den and John holding Katie's hand, and sitting on the bay. Now, he had something else to take care of.

– Chapter 34 –

UNCLE JOSS

As Jay struggled to run up the hill to the cottage, he could see in the distance that Joss was there ahead of him, almost at the little road that led to their cottage.

He shouted out to Joss, and the giant of a man stopped and turned around, waiting for him to come closer. Jay didn't want this man anywhere near his home or his family - it was all his own fault after all, he had caused it all with the stupid dreams and treasure hunting.

He was alone now, no-where to run or hide. He was already tired from running so far and from struggling with Den and John, and felt weak. Jay slowly approached Joss, out of breath, but not going too near. Joss laughed at him.

"I'm not afraid of you." Jay said, feeling very afraid.

"Then you're a fool." Came the reply with a laugh.

Joss was smirking. He cracked his huge knuckles and his broken teeth mocked him. Jay knew he was in for a beating, he wasn't sure if he could even survive at all, but he was not going to make it easy for Joss and he was not going to show any fear.

The very look of them was different – Jay carried his head up like a man with a backbone in him and he looked Joss full in the face. Jay met Joss' stare and for a second Joss' eyes flickered with uncertainty - he wasn't expecting defiance, but it passed, because it didn't matter.

Jay was looking about him for a weapon, a branch or rock, when he was suddenly punched hard in the side of the face, and then Joss was all over him. The first punch had hit him in the head like a steam train and he stumbled back. Then more powerful punches to the body.

Jay was struggling. He was kicking and punching this man-mountain back with all his strength, and although some of these hits were hurting him, it was only for a moment, then he came back twice as strong.

Joss was having fun. He had no compassion, no limits, and no line that he would not cross. He didn't even care about the treasure anymore; he just wanted to teach this boy a lesson. Joss was grunting and laughing and he was not going to stop.

Jay slipped to the floor and desperately reached out along the ground to find a rock, branch, anything, but he was kicked hard in the stomach and he rolled over, landing on his back. There was a large cut to his face which was putting blood into his eyes, making the madman just a red hazy blur lashing at him.

There was no-one left to help him, no-one to see him drift away from consciousness under the furious attack, but Katie was safe, Katie was safe.

Just as he thought it was the end, someone called out. At first he thought it was Joss, but no, because he had frozen mid-punch and was turning around. Jay couldn't see properly, he was dizzy, barely conscious and he could only see outlines through the blood in his eyes. He thought he heard Joss laugh but he wasn't sure.

Then he recognised the voice; then he knew it was Daniel.

"No, no." Jay tried to call out, "Danny run!"

But Joss turned back to him and kicked Jay so hard that he rolled down a steep gulley, rolling over and over until he landed at the base of a large tree. Joss turned to face the figure that had challenged him.

Jay couldn't see; couldn't stand. Pain tore through his body and the ground was swimming around him. A battle was going on; he could hear it, felt it through the shaking in the ground. Jay clung onto the trunk of the tree and tried to pull himself up to his feet. His ears and head were ringing from the howls of the fight and then, suddenly, silence.

Jay knew that Joss would be coming back to finish him off, he knew that he had to get his vision clear. He had to get to Daniel. He wiped the blood from his eyes and then gradually he started to focus until he saw Joss lying still in the dirt. Someone was standing over him. Jay pulled himself upright and clung onto the tree.

"Danny?" he managed to whisper "Is that you?"

"Who else?" said Daniel, running over to catch him from falling.

"How did you …. Did you bring an army or something?" Jay croaked,

"No," Daniel laughed, "we don't need an army – we got the marines!" Then Jay's eyes came into focus for just a moment, enough to see his big brother Marc in full marine combat gear standing over the bloodied and moaning Joss.

Jay smiled weakly then everything went black. Marc and Daniel caught him just as Jay's legs gave way and he collapsed. The last thing Jay heard was the distant sound of approaching sirens and Daniel saying,

"It's OK, we've got you"

– Chapter 35 –

THE SQUIRE'S DAUGHTER

(In the past – a few weeks before the storm).

The Squire's Manor house was located just outside the small port on a sprawling private estate. It was a large square building, with ten bedrooms, a great main hall and servants' quarters. The estate had stables and a small farm providing fresh food to the Squire and his guests.

On entering the Manor house, guests first arrived at the entrance hall where dead animals were paraded as trophies, a stuffed fox, forever twisted around, trying to snap at his own tail and half a dozen sea-birds staring with blank eyes in strange positions, and all loomed over by heads of sad stag and deer looking down forlornly at the visitors.

The great hall was the centrepiece of the house, originally designed for grand banquets and evenings of dancing; but the Squire used it as an office and court where he presided over his men and staff.

The Squire was married to a plain, timid woman, who had brought a huge fortune with her when they married, and apart from providing one daughter and the face of respectability for the Squire, he had no other interest in her.

Their daughter was a beautiful young woman aged seventeen, named Genefer, but far from being loved by the Squire, she was regarded as property, to be married off and sold to the richest and most powerful man available.

The most eligible bachelor in the whole of Cornwall at that time was Lord Trevalon, a cruel, vain older man, known for drinking and hunting. He was under pressure to marry to continue the family name, and had made a very lucrative deal with the Squire to marry his daughter. Genefer was of course, horrified and scared, but would not dare to disobey her very powerful father.

Genefer was crying in her room. Her maid Phillida was trying to console her, but with the impending arranged marriage only three months away, Genefer was desperate, and unable to see any way to escape this terrible marriage. If she tried to refuse, her powerful and corrupt father had promised to throw her in jail, and as the local magistrate it was not an empty threat, he could even have her hanged if he wanted.

Genefer and Phillida were physically very similar, same age, build and with long wavy hair, but the most striking difference between them, were their eyes, Genefer with light blue eyes and Phillida with deep green eyes. Phillida knew Genefer's secret – her mistress was in love with one of the Squire's men, Guy.

Guy, tall, black hair, dark blue eyes, straight back, strong arms with a wide white smile, worked for the Squire as a customs man, sometimes acting within the law and sometimes not so much, whatever the Squire ordered.

Phillida had devised a plan to help her mistress to escape the marriage, and that rainy afternoon, they sat together as the maid told her mistress her idea. If they waited for the next storm when a ship was in trouble, then that would act as a cover for them to escape from the Manor, which would normally be heavily guarded.

They would wear identical shawls and bonnets, so that people who saw them would not know which was servant and which was mistress. They would meet Guy, and then her mistress would be free to run away to London with him, and they could live on her collection of fine jewels and diamonds.

Meanwhile as a distraction, Phillida would take a pony trap to Liskeard and then be seen buying a ticket to Plymouth. People would remember her dressed in her Mistresses fine blue silk dress travelling to Plymouth, and she would then change back into plain clothes and take another coach back to the town and let the Master know that his daughter had run away to Plymouth.

Genefer listened to this plan with horror. It was far too dangerous, she had never disobeyed her father in her whole life, and she had no doubts as to the extent of his fury if she spoiled his plans to inherit a fortune from the arranged marriage. She was equally terrified for her maid, who would most certainly be hanged if she was ever caught or suspected of aiding this crazy plan. She said no, definitely no.

As the days past, and Phillida repeated her plan over and over, the seed of the idea began to take root. Following a visit from Guy who was desperate to marry her, and excited by the chance to steal her away, Genefer gradually began to consider the idea.

One week later, it was agreed. A storm was in the air, and the locals knew that the weather was turning. There was a churning in the salt air that warned of breaking weather. The sky turned dark grey, and the black water surged heavily around the jagged harbour cliff.

– Chapter 36 –

BREAK FOR FREEDOM

(In the past - on the night of the storm)

Shipwreck was such a common event on the Cornish coastline, that the young lovers did not have too long to wait before a vicious storm crashed onto the shoreline one night, and tore a ship into three pieces, and then smashed it against the rocks.

All who could render assistance were out of their beds helping the sailors and fishermen. The wind roared and the angry sea rumbled and churned. The air was filled with the shouts of the fishermen trying to secure their boats, and the screams of the women and children in the darkness.

The Squire had sent all his men out to salvage anything of value from the ship, with instructions not to waste time rescuing anyone.

Phillida ran to her mistresses' room, and found her stuffing all of her valuable jewellery and precious stones into a travel case. Quickly Phillida put on Genefer's bright blue silk dress, and Genefer changed into a plain rough dress which she had taken from one of the servants a few days earlier. Giggling madly, they both covered themselves in long black shawls with black bonnets to cover their faces – at the same height and build, they looked identical.

The two young women easily slipped out of the Manor house unseen, normally challenged by staff or guards, but not tonight when the Squire's money was at stake - everyone was out trying to recover as much as possible from the ship.

Bonnets pulled tightly over their faces, they ran through the rain soaked pebbled streets. The little were alleys busy with people out in the night looking for loved ones or heading towards the beach, no-one noticed them scurry by as they headed out to the end of the rocks at the far end of the beach.

Genefer was shocked by the scenes; she had never left the Manor house during a ship wreck before, and had no idea how terrible it could be. But Phillida kept pulling her on, not allowing her stop and help.

Clambering across the black, slippery rocks they could see the outline ahead of Guy, huddled against the rain, with a background of flashing lightning and rolling black clouds. Genefer ran the last few yards to him and they fell into each other arms at the very tip of the high rocks, and kissed against the backdrop of the crashing waves.

Phillida put the jewellery case down and went up to the couple.

"Genefer" she called against the sound of the rushing gale, "I need to say something to you in private before you leave." Guy stepped back to allow Phillida to go up close to whisper in Genefer's ear.

Genefer smiled at her loving maid, but as Phillida leaned close to her, instead of whispering, she shoved her with great force over the edge of the cliff and onto the crashing ocean and rocks below in the blackness.

Guy ran up to Phillida and shouted,

"I didn't believe you would actually do it!" he laughed, and they held each other and danced and laughed in front of the angry bright moon.

"It's all ours," said Phillida, "it's a fortune in jewels. She will be smashed on the rocks in her poor dress and no-one will look for her. So many bodies, it's perfect."

Phillida removed a diamond necklace and earrings from the bag and put them on. Laughing loudly she danced on the slippery, jagged rocks.

Guy hugged her; he had the most beautiful, clever girl in the world and a fortune to start his life again in London. He had safely hidden the gold that he had stolen from the cave where no-one would ever find it, after stealing from those idiots Jack and Matt – he would tell Phillida about the gold on their honeymoon. What more could he ask for?

He laughed at the storm, and as he turned around to hold Phillida once more, he was too late to prevent her from crashing a large rock down upon his head, and then as he staggered back, he looked at her with shock and sadness as she kicked him over the edge of the rocks to join Genefer at the bottom of the sea.

Phillida sat down on the soaking wet rocks and hugged the bag of jewels. She laughed and rocked and hummed a little tune, as the wind and rain howled in disgust at her murderous ways.

– Chapter 37 –

WHAT PHILLIDA DID NEXT

After spending a few hours in her cottage, and changing back into her servant's clothes, Phillida approached the Manor house to complete her plan. Lanterns burned in every window and the Squires men were rushing about, in and around the house.

She slipped past them all as they had no time for a servant girl, and she managed to get into the main hall where the Squire was standing with his back to the room, staring into a roaring fire.

She stood very still, unwilling to speak without permission; she patiently waited for him to become aware of her. Unknown to her, he knew exactly who was there, but was waiting to see if she would dare speak first.

There they stood, outside men were shouting and running around, and inside the great fire crackled and popped. Finally, without turning or moving, the squire said,

"What d'ya want girl?"

"Squire," she said quickly "I have saved your daughter's fortune for you."

He turned around so fast that she stepped back in surprise. He stared at her, the beautiful servant girl with bright green eyes, soaking wet from the rain and showing no real fear of him even though he held her life in his hands. She was clutching a travelling bag.

He strode over to her with two large strides and snatched the bag from her hands, she was not expecting this and let go, the bag falling open, and the contents scattered all over the wooden floor.

In the firelight and candlelight, the room lit up with reflections of rubies, emeralds, sapphires and diamonds, dancing around the room like bright coloured sparks.

The two people remained standing, frozen.

"Pick them up girl!" he ordered. Phillida quickly scooped up all the jewels and put them back into the bag and handed them to the squire.

"I'm sorry sir," she said "but the mistress was wearing the diamond necklace and earrings, I wasn't able to take them back off her, she has taken the coach to Plymouth, I jumped off to bring you back the rest of your jewels."

The Squire took this information in. She waited, expecting anger. But he took the bag and looked into it for some time. Eventually he reached inside and brought out a gold ring with a diamond in the centre. He turned it over in his hand, then held it out to Phillida and said,

"Take this." Phillida tried to speak but he waved her away, and then strode out of the great hall.

Phillida put the ring on her finger and admired it and smiled. She had a small fortune in diamonds now the trust of the Squire, who knows where that may lead? And Phillida hummed her little tune again.

Chapter 38

GRANFER NANKIVELL

(In the past - on the night of the storm)

Like many farmers and dwellers living near to the sea, Granfer Nankivell was wakened by neighbours who told him of the wreck in the port. He hooked up his donkey cart, and set out on the seven mile trek in the blackness of night to see if he could help in any way, and then to see if there was anything left of the ship and cargo that he could salvage.

As the donkey's hooves clipped along the country lanes, he could hear men and women in all the other lanes, making their way down to the port in the darkness. The heavy rain had now reduced to a drenching sheet rain, and this in turn would subside further as the night continued, but too late for the lost souls from the stricken ship.

Arriving at the small port, Granfer Nankivell left his donkey and cart nearby, and joined the busy throng of people coming and going like busy worker ants. Dead bodies were being carried gently into the pilchard huts, and locals were scattered collecting anything washed ashore from the stricken ship that was strewn across the beach.

Not being a very assuming man, Granfer went to the far edge of the beach, and after checking that no man or beast were in need of his rescue, he started to beach comb for anything useful, and was excited to find a few pewter plates and spoons, and some torn silk which had been ripped from a bale thrown into the sea by the storm.

He could see more silk floating on the edge of the water, and despite the freezing cold of the water and rain, he waded out because he wanted Grannie Nankivell to have silk after a lifetime of working on the farm and taking care of him and their five fine sons.

With one hand clinging to the stone wall, he leaned in and pulled at the silk, but was horrified to find that far from being a bale of silk, it was in fact the body of a young woman dressed in a simple poor dress.

He waded in and took hold of her, trying to call for help, but with the high winds and bustling people on the beach, no one heard him. With every last drop of energy left in him, he pulled her ashore and sat down to recover from this effort with her head resting on his leg. He made a sign of the cross and started to say a silent prayer for the loss of such youth and beauty.

It was then that she moved, and coughed and as he turned her over, she threw up all the seawater in her lungs and lay gasping on the wet sand.

Quickly Granfer took off his jacket and wrapped it around her as she was shivering and crying. Genefer did not move away from the man who had rescued her, she was grateful, but did not wish to live.

The man she loved had betrayed her. The friend she loved had stolen him and her fortune and then tried to murder her. Her father, who should be her protector, wanted her married for money or thrown away, and now with her fortune lost, she would never dare return to him. No, she wished only to lie there on that beach and die.

"Are yee from ship or toon?" Granfer asked kindly.

But Genefer just shook her head.

"What's yee name cheeld?" Granfer asked.

Genefer said the first thing that came into her head, the name of her favourite doll from childhood,

"Polly" she whispered. "I have no family or home. All I had was lost on the ship. I am no-one. I have no-one." And she started to cry again.

"Theer, theer," the old man said, "I have a small farm near, yee can come and get well and then help my wife with the chores?"

Genefer looked at him, such a kindly face, but she could not stop sobbing and shaking,

"Theer, theer," the old man said again, "I wish you wudden, I do sure 'nough."

He hesitated "we don't have much, but we are good God-fearing folk. I can take 'ee there now and if not to yeer liking, then I will bring yee back in the morn."

Genefer nodded, she had no choice. The Squire's men would be looking for her; she had nowhere else to go.

Later that night, a wet and sad girl arrived at the little farm. Grannie Nankivell made her a smoking bowl of broth and dried her clothes on a warm red peat and furze fire.

Grannie Nankivell was a quick little woman with twinkling dark eyes, who wore a black cottage-bonnet over a neat cap, a blue print apron, black dress and shawl. She had a warm smile and Genefer felt safe in the little cottage.

When the morning broke over the beautiful landscape, and the hopeful bright sun shone over the farm, Polly managed to smile as she stepped outside to look around in the daylight.

Granfer and Grannies home was along a little lane that stood nearby to other little cottages dotted along the hillside. Elms and oaks bent over them lovingly, with apple trees growing thickly in the adjoining orchards. The clear light fell directly upon the farmhouse and all that side of the valley and its flocks of sheep.

Polly did not return to town the next morning, nor the morning after that. In fact Polly stayed at the farm, milking cows, feeding chickens and doing chores for the family.

After two years she married the youngest of the five fine sons and they had seven fine children. Polly never left the farm, and was happy and content for the rest of her long and peaceful life

– Chapter 39 –

WHAT NOW?

(Back in the present time)

After a trip to the hospital to bandage Jay's injuries and then giving a statement to the Police about Uncle Joss, the five Pengelli children sat around the smouldering coal fire in the Cornish cottage. Tricia had gone to bed with a headache after shouting at them for being so irresponsible.

Marc and Natasha were both in shock at the whole episode. Marc, who had been in war zones, had never heard anything like it. Natasha, as a cynical and clever sixteen year old didn't really believe any of it at all.

Despite their builds being completely different, it was clear that Marc and Natasha were brother and sister. Their face shape and cheek bones were the same and they shared deep brown eyes and dark brown hair – even though Marc's was shaved quite close and Natasha's was long, straight and glossy.

They were both quite different to Jay and Daniel in personality, more independent and focused on their own individual futures, while Jay and Daniel were very much family focused, perhaps because they were the ones left behind to help Tricia through all the financial and personal problems.

Marc was silent; Natasha shook her head and muttered angrily:

"Idiots!"

Jay glared at her, Daniel shrugged, and Katie giggled.

Jay was warming himself in front of the fire, the flames lighting up his face in orange and red. The top of his head had stitches and a bandage, his ribs were bruised and there was a long cut to his leg. He winced with pain as he shifted position on the floor to try to get comfortable.

He was well aware that he had failed to find the gold; he had found the rubies and then lost them, put everyone in danger and taken a beating. Not a particularly brilliant outcome. He sighed.

"Now what?" said Jay finally.

"Now nothing!" Natasha snapped scornfully, "I don't know what's been going on, but Mum's upset and some nutter has beaten you up and another nutter kidnapped Katie, isn't that enough?"

Jay knew she was right, and didn't really have anything to say in his defence.

Later that evening when Natasha had carried the sleeping Katie to bed, Marc, Daniel and Jay remained silently in front of the warm glowing fire, drinking hot chocolate.

Jay hadn't noticed before how old Marc had become. His big brother was now a grown man who fought overseas and lived this whole separate life to the rest of the family.

Daniel was thoughtful; he was always the one who worried the most, the word of caution. Even now he was fighting back the urge to tell Jay what an irresponsible idiot he had been. He looked at Jay.

Jay half smiled and knew exactly was Daniel was thinking, because he had told him often enough before.

Marc and Daniel eventually drifted off to bed, but Jay remained staring at the fire until his eyes were burning from the hot embers. What had it all been for? He had these new crazy powers to go in and out of the past, and now banned from using them. He nearly lost Katie twice; he lost the rubies, got beaten up and didn't find any gold.

It all came down to the gold. Jay wanted it so badly. Not for him – it had never been about him – it was about all the debt chasers who had made his mother cry, it was about his family losing their beloved house in London, and their friends and everything that was safe and familiar. No, it was still all about the gold.

"So," he said quietly to the fire "I had better go and find the gold."

– Chapter 40 –

ONE LAST DREAM

Jay rose early just as the dawn was starting and limped down the cobbled streets towards Rum Cove, where he knew the gold had been hidden by Jack and Matt. He wanted to see who took the gold and where they hid it next, because there was just a slim chance that it was still lying around somewhere waiting for Jay to find it.

The tide was going out and the sand was wet and hard. As Jay approached the entrance to the cave, seagulls swirled above him, circling in the hope of finding something for breakfast. He sat on the rock at the entrance to rest because his leg was hurting and so were his ribs and head. He had been ordered bed rest by the hospital, but Jay had never been very good at taking advice.

Closing his eyes he concentrated on the scene when Jack and Matt were hiding the gold in the wall of the cave. In his imagination he then thought about them leaving the cave, and he then thought about the shadowy figure coming to take the gold away.

Nothing happened. He was too awake to sleep, and for some reason he was unable to jump into the dream like he did before. Angry and frustrated he picked up a small rock and threw it, smashing it into the side of the cave, and then without warning, he was suddenly dropping backwards into the dream.

He was falling at great speed in darkness, desperately throwing his arms about he tried to find something to grab hold of, but he was just tumbling through the air. As he was falling, he started to hear faint sounds – men's voices, the clip clop of ponies on stones, the wash of the sea, seagulls and then he knew he was approaching the scene. There was complete silence for a fraction of a second and then he suddenly arrived back in the dream…

It was loud and busy, men and women, horses and ponies, all taking kegs and silks up and down the little pathways.

The Squire's men were shouting orders, riding around on sweating horses, and making sure that the valuables were loaded into the Squire's pony carts. While this was going on, the Squire sat still on top of a powerful black horse, just watching as everything was unloaded and transported.

Jack and Matt were standing near the shore directing the locals. They said very little, just a wave of the hand, or a nod of the head, and the men and women hurried along to do as they were bid. One man tripped and dropped a bale of silk onto the wet sand and then ran as Matt tried to kick him for his clumsiness.

Jay found himself high up on the side of the rocks where he could look down on the scene, which reminded him of a movie set. He was cold, tired and in pain, and he just wanted to find the gold quickly and then go home to rest.

He saw the gold bags slip from the back of one of the Squire's horses, it was so quick that it was almost unnoticeable, but Jack and Matt who were the nearest to the water's edge saw it happen and they nudged each other but did not move. They took a risk and just waited.

The Squire and his men took off, and then Jay watched the cutter leave to escape the Excise men's boat. The people of the town vanished like smoke being blown away by a silent breeze and he saw that the beach was now empty except for Jack and Matt.

When Jack and Matt thought that all was clear, the two men laughed out loud and waded out to the spot where the bags fell, not thinking for a moment that they would be full of gold. They dragged the bags out of the sea laughing and cursing. They looked even nastier when drenched with sea-water, their dark heavy clothes weighing them down, with their boots squelching on the stones.

Dragging the bags into the caves they shoved and pushed each other, their laughter coarse and loud. Jay watched them with disgust, 'not men' he thought 'just big ugly vicious kids'.

They were so noisy and engrossed in their own good fortune that they did not even notice the third man watching them from the entrance to the cave, but this time Jay did. He watched as Guy hid and observed in silence.

Chapter 41

RAINBOWS END

Jack and Matt eventually left the cave, heading straight for the Inn to sample the freshly delivered rum to celebrate their huge find, and to toast the Squire's men for their stupidity.

Guy quickly opened the space in the wall of the cave and found the bags of gold. He did not jump around and laugh and curse like the other two smugglers, he merely smiled, as though finding the gold was bound to happen to him – he expected life to hand him good fortune.

He called out to an old man who was just on his way home leading a pony and cart.

"Hey you, I need your cart for the Squire!" The old man stopped and looked at the well-dressed young man. He didn't want to hand over his precious pony and cart. Usually Guy would have ordered him to, but rather than make a scene he said,

"Here, this is for you, I just need it for a short time." He handed the man a pile of coins. The man looked at the money with surprise, a week's wages and more. He took the money but still watched the young man, something about him that made the old man hesitate.

Guy took the tatty leather reigns from the old man, who still remained standing there. Guy pointed up to the top of the hill,

"Come and collect him later," he said, "from the Squire's Manor house."

The old man put the money in his pocket, and then he patted the pony,

"Just point 'im right way and tell 'im "home" and hee'll come home by hisself." He said, and then he walked off towards the Inn to also sample the newly arrived rum with his newfound fortune.

Jay groaned as he saw Guy load the bags of gold onto the cart, leap up, and click the reins to make the pony walk on. Jay was already limping, he knew chasing after a pony and cart uphill wasn't going to be easy, but then, what was in his world these days?

Once Jay could see where the cart was going he was able to slow down. The long upward journey to the Squire's Manor was just one road, and Guy did not seem to be in any particular hurry, he casually leaned back, gazing at the scenery as the sun set on the beautiful cove.

Jay dragged himself up the winding streets until he could see up ahead the long drive into the Squires estate. As the cart travelled on ahead, Jay saw the cartwheel hit a rock and tip for a moment almost throwing Guy off sideways, but although he managed to stay on board, one of the gold coins slipped out of the back of the cart and rolled down into the roots of an oak tree.

Guy did not notice, or did not care, and carried on up to the big house. As Jay passed the giant tree, he leaned down and picked up the shiny gold coin and put it into his pocket.

It was almost completely dark when Jay finally followed the pony and cart to the back of the Manor House. He found Guy hauling the bags towards the open trap door of a cellar that led down into the Squire's stores under the great house.

When he had unloaded the bags, he smacked the hind legs of the little pony and said,

"Home!" and sure enough, the little pony obediently pulled the empty cart by himself, and set off back to the old man.

Guy left the bags on the grass and climbed down the ladder. A light was shining up from below, and he could hear Guy talking to someone down there.

"This is the last now, you can get back to your chores, and I'll finish here." Whoever he had been speaking to must have left the cellar, because he heard the door slam.

As Jay waited behind a bush next to the house, he watched as Guy dragged the bags one at a time down the wooden ladder into the underground store.

Jay was in pain and shifted to try to get more comfortable, causing a twig to snap under him, and within a second, Guys head shot out from the cellar door and looked around. Dizziness was threatening to knock Jay off balance, but luckily a pretty kitchen servant was passing by at that moment carrying a large jug of cream.

"Looking for me?" Guy called out grinning. The servant's face turned bright pink and she ran away. Guy laughed, making a mental note to find out her name later. He forgot all about the twig snapping and climbed back down the ladder whistling.

Jay could hear dragging noises from below, and decided that he had to take the chance to see what Guy was up to. As he peered *down, he could see that the lit cellar was full of kegs of rum, bales of silk and countless stacks of valuables and paintings.*

It was obviously the Squire's treasure store. Guy was dragging barrels away from an old fireplace. He pulled out the front irons of the grate and stuffed the bags of gold in there – in with the other valuables that he had been stealing over time.

He replaced the fire grates, pulled the barrels back in front and then climbed back up the ladder. Jay lay perfectly still as Guy pulled the trap door closed and bolted the cellar door from the inside. Jay had finally found the location of the gold at the end of the rainbow.

It was a perfect hiding place right under the Squire's nose; he would never think to look for the stolen goods hidden in his own store room. This meant that unless Guy had come back for the gold, then it would probably still be hidden there. After all these years, Jay could just go there and take it back.

– Chapter 42 –

THE MANOR HOUSE

Dizziness from the cold and pain eventually caught up with Jay and he must have passed out, and then this somehow woke him up from the dream.

He was back on the sand in the cave, and some young children were now nearby, laughing and making a sandcastle and that kept falling down.

Jay checked the time, it was 9.15 am. He sent a text to Daniel,

'Found where gold hidden. Meet me at top of Manor Rd.' There was only a brief delay, before he read the reply,

'No way! Be there in15'

Jay then realised that he now had to climb all the way back up the hill again! The bus only ran once an hour and he had already missed it, so he slowly started to limp back up to Manor Road and just hoped that for once, it didn't rain in Cornwall.

It started to rain. Not a huge storm or anything like that, but a miserable grey drizzle, that relentlessly fell from the sky and gradually soaked every part of him.

By the time Jay reached the entrance to the estate on Manor Road he was shivering uncontrollably, and aware that actually he was in trouble. He needed painkillers and warmth and sleep, none of which were immediately available to him.

He groaned as he slowly lowered himself under the great oak tree for some shelter from the rain, and it was then that he remembered the gold coin. He put his hand in his pocket, it was empty, but then realised that it was back in the dream. Still, he dug down in the roots of the tree with his penknife, and managed to smile through the pain when he found the muddy gold coin, still waiting for him after all these years.

Marc sped up in his car, and Daniel jumped out with a heavy raincoat for Jay that he made him put on. Jay smiled; Daniel could be such an old woman.

"You're supposed to be sick." Daniel muttered, "Still trying to get yourself killed?"

Jay shrugged,

"Guess so." but he was grateful for the warm coat.

Marc, Daniel and Jay started to walk up the long winding road to the Manor house. Jay filled them in as they walked, and he told them about the gold coin. Just when they were all starting to feel quite excited about the gold, they turned the corner and the Manor House came into full view. Then their smiles dropped.

The Manor House was still standing. It was still a large, grey imposing building, still occupied and beautifully maintained …but - and it was a mighty big but – whoever lived there now really believed in high security.

There was an eight foot perimeter fence all around the building. Security cameras on every corner of the house, and men in uniforms with ferocious guard dogs were patrolling around.

Daniel whistled,

"Who lives here now, the head of MI5?" he exclaimed.

Jay was speechless, just another impossible obstacle.

Marc was carefully studying the whole set up.

"This is hard core." he said finally, "Full on top security, hi-tech cameras, probably motion activated laser sensors, and those guys look like they're armed. Forget it." He shook his head and turned around to walk back.

Deciding that it was probably best not to be seen by the guards, the boys followed Marc back to the car.

Jay stopped. He stood there in the rain, soaked, bruised, dizzy and desolate. He took the gold coin out of his pocket with his shaking cold fingers and showed it to Daniel,

"Look" he said, "I found gold."

Daniel put his hand on his brother's shoulder,

"Yeah mate, you did." He said smiling.

Chapter 43

TRICIA

The boy's mother was waiting for them all at the cottage; it was clear from her expression that she had been talking to Katie about the past few days.

"OK enough!" Tricia Pengelli screamed at her children, "let's go and see what your father has to say about all this!"

All five children sighed simultaneously. Every time there was a crisis, they were all hauled off to the hospital to explain to their father (in his coma) what they had been up to.

Well, it made her happy so they went. They arrived in the coma ward and went into his room, where as usual he lay perfectly still in his hospital bed. Usually she would greet him, kiss him and tell him all the news and get the children to speak to him, but not this time.

"Well!" she exclaimed loudly "I want you all to look at your father's broken bones and all the scars on his face from the crash!"

Katie was scared and grasped Daniel's hand.

"What do you mean?" Jay asked.

"What I say!" she was becoming angrier. They all looked.

Daniel stated the obvious,

"He didn't break any bones." and they could all see that there weren't any scars.

"And why is that?" she demanded "<u>Why</u>!?

Katie started to cry.

"What are you doing?" Jay asked his mother, picking up Katie to stop her crying.

"What am I doing?" she demanded, "No, what are <u>you</u> doing?"

She was so angry. They didn't know what to do. They waited a moment, and then she sat down sadly,

"Don't you know?" she asked quietly. They all shrugged, too scared to speak.

"Your father was never in a car crash."

The impact of this statement hit the five of them like a steam train; they all knew what she was about to say next,

"He just never came back from his dream."

Chapter 44

JAY

Back home, Natasha and Tricia remained furious. Jay tried to explain that they needed to find their Dad, but Tricia stormed off slamming doors. He turned to Natasha,

"You don't understand," he pleaded, "if Dad is lost, we should try to find him!"

"But he's not lost though is he?" she scoffed, "He's in the flippin' hospital!" and then she scowled at them all and left, also slamming the door.

The three brothers sat up most of the night talking about the situation. Both Daniel and Marc thought that it would be too dangerous to carry on.

Finding out that their Dad had been lost in dreams for three years had been the biggest shock of all. Peter Pengelli had somehow stumbled across a link to the past as well, and travelled there in his dreams, and was now unable to find his way back.

Perhaps he went without any back up, perhaps it was his first trip and he didn't know how to come back. But then, how did Tricia know all about it? Why hadn't she tried to find him? Had she gone to see the witch, if so, why hadn't the witch told them? None of it made any sense.

After Marc and Daniel had gone to bed, Jay walked alone down to the cliffs. He was chilled with the early morning air, but as he approached the rocks, the morning sunrise started to emerge on the sea's horizon.

Jay now loved the sounds of the waves as they washed in and out on the shore, and the circling seagulls were familiar and friendly. Cornwall had been in his blood all along, and now he was beginning to feel that he belonged here.

He climbed to the very edge of the rocky cliffs to the spot where Guy and Phillida were thrown into the pounding waves, and he looked down at the beauty and danger of the crashing sea. Sitting on the edge of the rocks, the sun slowly emerged as a truly beautiful bright orange semi-circle, gradually lighting the sky as it silently rose from the very edge of the world.

Jay hadn't seen Den since they had rescued Katie, and he missed his buddy. The rubies were on their way to who knows where by now, and he couldn't even prove that they existed in the first place, and it would seem that all Bonnie did was to take Katie for a plate of chips!

Remembering the heated discussions from the night before, Jay shook his head and sighed. Daniel had wanted to know if there was any way to rescue his Dad without any risk - there wasn't. The idea that their Mum could lose another of her family to these dreams was unthinkable, even though his Dad remained lost somewhere in a far off dream.

Marc was dead set against any kind of attempt to retrieve the gold from the high security house, and had banged his fist on the coffee table in anger at the very suggestion of it.

'I should stop now,' Jay thought, 'before anyone else gets hurt. It would be the most responsible and sensible thing to do.'

Jay turned the gold coin over in his hand. He had polished it to a brilliant shine, and the feel and colour of it was just amazing.

So, should he just go back to normal life now, study for his exams, and help out Mum in the cottage? Or should he carry on searching in secret and practicing his dream-jumping on his own? He could then try to find his Dad, and even check out the Manor house - who lives there now, and is there any way to retrieve the gold?

He shifted his position on the rocks, he was still in pain and covered in bandages and stitches, he would have to be a complete and utter idiot to continue with these dangerous ideas.

"Perhaps I should decide by tossing a coin." He said to himself,

"Heads I stop now and forget it all, or Tails I wait until I have recovered and feel stronger, and then I carry on alone."

Jay held the gold coin up and then tossed it high into the air.

As it tumbled up towards the sky, the sun reflected the solid gold into brilliant flashes that danced in the air until it hurt his eyes. He held out his hand to catch it as it landed, and then looked down at the gold coin resting in his palm.

Jay smiled.

End.

Coming soon

Book 2

WRECKER JACK

BLACK SKY